Miller and Kelby

Major case squad files: a collection of short stories

Miller and Kelby

Major case squad files: a collection of short stories

by Maxine Flam

Chapeltown Books

British Library Cataloguing in Publication Data
A Record of this Publication is available from the British Library

ISBN 978-1-915762-27-6

This edition published 2025 by Chapeltown Books
Manchester, England

Cover design © Peter Shovlin

Dedicated to Dr. Mike, my medical advisor, who encouraged me to write and to continue to submit despite all the rejections.

Contents

Preface

Just who are Joseph (Joe) Miller and William (Bill) Kelby?

They are two men who are partners and work for the Los Angeles Police Department Major Case Squad during the late 1970s.

Joe Miller is 32, 6'0", 175 pounds, brown hair, and blue eyes. He is married with two young children. He started to work for the L.A.P.D. as a patrol officer twelve years prior and rose rapidly in the ranks to become the youngest detective to join the Major Case Squad at the age of twenty-five. His first partner was a senior detective who taught Miller all he could before he retired two years later. Miller was then paired with his current partner, Bill Kelby.

Bill Kelby is slightly younger. He is 30 years old, 6'1", 170 pounds, brown hair, and brown eyes. He is married with two small children. He graduated third in his class at the police academy, starting as a motorcycle officer at the age of 18. He studied hard and moved up in the ranks to become a detective at twenty-five. He was partnered with Joe Miller. Miller and Kelby think alike and play off of each other while investigating cases but Miller is the senior officer.

Because Miller and Kelby Crime Stories take place in the 1970s, there are none of the modern conveniences available today: no DNA, no cellphones, and computers were large mainframes. It was a time when police work was done the old-fashioned way: through hard work, grit, and determination. Detectives used fingerprints as they sifted through evidence and large computer printouts to track down a criminal. Staking-out a location, sometimes all night, at the sacrifice of their own families, was what detectives did. Go back in time to when detectives had to dig a little deeper and take more risks to find the evidence they needed to arrest the criminals.

Six Murders and Counting

How did I end up here? What time is it? Oh, not again… *This can't be… Is she dead?… I gotta get the hell out of here before someone finds me with this person, whoever she is.* George picked his clothes up off the floor, got dressed, and walked out. No one in the building saw or heard him. It was five in the morning; everyone was asleep. That was fortunate for him but not for the victim. *I need to figure out what happened. Who is this woman? Why does this keep happening? I don't understand.*

George arrived at his apartment, stripped, and took a long hot shower. There was some blood on his shirt. *I better throw the clothes out. I'll put everything in a garbage bag and drop it in the can in the alley. Today is garbage day. I can't have anyone thinking that I had anything to do with this because I didn't. What happened??? Come on… think… I left work yesterday and awoke in this woman's bed. But she's dead… who did it?… That's it. Someone got into the apartment and killed the woman. Maybe it was a jealous boyfriend or husband? He left me alone. Phew… lucky… I didn't know her. I don't know how I got in her bed. I'm going to have breakfast, dress for work, and go into work like nothing is wrong because there is nothing wrong. I didn't do anything wrong.*

George decided not to worry about it. *Someone else did it and the police will find that person. But what about the other people? There are so many more. Everywhere I go… It must be a coincidence. Yes, that's what it is… a coincidence. I was at the wrong place at the wrong time.*

"Someone must have seen something," said exasperated Detective Joe Miller of the Major Case Squad to his partner Bill Kelby at the scene of the latest murder.

"No one saw anything at any of the other murders. So why should this be any different?" replied Kelby.

The bed was covered in blood and a 6" hunting knife was stuck in the back of the latest victim. All the details were the same. Each body was nude – no struggle. There was what looked like semen on the dead woman's back. "Call forensics and see what they can come up with: perhaps some fingerprints, anything we can use to nail this psycho and ask them to check if this is semen like the others victims," said Miller.

"How can this happen without anyone seeing something? Would you please explain it to me?" replied Kelby.

"Oh, someone saw something; the murderer saw something. This is so damn frustrating," said Miller. "He must be covered in blood. How did he walk out of here unnoticed? There aren't any bloody footprints. What did he do? Fly across the room?"

"Maybe he brought a change of clothes in a suitcase?" said Kelby. "Come on, be serious."

"Now don't be funny. Seriously, where are the

bloody clothes? He didn't wash them or leave them behind. What'd he do with them? Bring a garbage bag in his pocket. There isn't any blood in the shower. How'd he kill them and not get blood on himself?... It makes no sense." Miller shook his head. "Unless, he murders them while he was nude. Of course, that's it! His clothes are on a chair or the floor. After he kills them, he dresses and leaves. That's why there isn't any blood anywhere else. Maybe there's some on his body but he showers when he arrives home and tosses the clothes in the garbage. We're dealing with a sicko."

"You're just figuring that out now. This makes five dead bodies and we're no closer to solving this serial killer than we were on the first murder. Different parts of town, different people, different races, and sexes. I'd like to know where they met. In an era of the swinging 70s' disco, this twisted person has his pick of places and people. Seriously, this person must be out of his mind," stated Kelby.

"This is out of our league. We need to consult the department psychologist on this one as soon as possible," said Miller.

"Let's go see Dr. Delmonico," replied Kelby.

"Well, after reviewing the autopsies and evidence collected, what you have here, in my expert opinion, is two different personalities inhabiting the same body of the killer," said Dr. Delmonico. "One may know the other exists or then again may not. But you better find this person soon or he'll kill again and again. You're up to five. I suspect this isn't new. He's probably been killing in other cities. You need to put this on the wire and find out if any place has had a string of unsolved killings that don't match a pattern."

"Are you out of your mind? Do you know how many places there are to contact?" shouted Miller.

"Then you better get started because you haven't seen anything yet. If this is a repressive personality disorder, and I think it is, then the killer rears its ugly head after having a stressful day. But, back to the murders at hand... let's assume for a moment, he works for a tyrant or lives with a dominant parent or partner, one that abuses him mentally and physically. Let's also assume he is a submissive personality which means he takes the abuse. The boss puts him down or the mother yells at him for being late or his girlfriend or boyfriend says he can't do anything right. 'You lazy, good for nothing so and so,' someone says for example. Whatever it is, he can't speak up for himself. The dominant personality comes out. He goes to bars, dances, discos, wherever, and mingles. Wherever people congregate, he's the life of the party. He isn't a bad-looking person. I'd even bet he's nice-looking. He's probably a good conversationalist with a fun personality, as five people found out when they asked him back to their place for sex. That's the key. He goes back to their place, never his. He goes with anyone. It doesn't matter the race or sex. Of the five dead people, four are women: Black, Hispanic, Asian, Filipina, and one white man. So far, four of the people were traced back to nightclubs and bars in the area. The man was a prostitute. Maybe that was a spur-of-the-moment thing because he couldn't find someone to hook-up with in the bar." Dr. Delmonico stopped speaking and looked at the detectives for a moment.

"We checked the flophouse where the man was found dead. They rent by the hour. The flophouse manager was so drunk he didn't know who was coming or going," said Kelby.

"We've interviewed all the places where the dead people visited and we came up empty," said Miller.

"Well, go back and interview them again," continued Dr. Delmonico. "Now you have a fifth person to add to the list. This suspect is an equal-opportunity killer. The only statistics I can give you about him is he's probably on the taller side because he has been able to subdue his victims. I'd say maybe 6' tall. Based on what I've read, he ties them up mostly with rope and stuffs a tie or ascot in their mouth so they can't scream. It takes strength to hold someone down, to bind their arms and legs, and shove a knife in their back. He had sex with each victim with no condom before killing them. One more thing…"

"More bad news?" replied Kelby.

"After he shoves the knife in the back of his victim, he has a second orgasm. Forensics confirmed it with all five of the victims. For him, it's a better release if you will. Killing them completes the sex act for him. I believe after the second orgasm he changes back to the submissive personality," said Delmonico confidently.

"Christ, not a dominant fetish," said Miller rolling his eyes.

"He has sex with them; they roll over, and go to sleep. He ties them up, murders them, and gets off on it. Terrific… it's worse than kinky," said Kelby.

George went to work as if nothing had happened the night before.

"Hey Georgie," said a co-worker who walked over to his desk.

"I asked you not to call me that," replied George.

"The boss wants to see you."

George got up from his chair and walked into the boss's office.

"Close the door, George. I reviewed your work and found it to be subpar. Why don't you follow company policy?" George stared at his boss like he wasn't there while his boss droned on and on about what a poor worker he was. "Maybe you should consider transferring back to the home office? Have I made myself clear?" said the boss.

"Yes sir, I understand?"

George emerged from the boss's office with his head bowed low. Everybody looked at him while they tried not to laugh.

He went back to his cubicle and worked through lunch so he could leave early.

Four o'clock couldn't come fast enough. George left. *Thank God, I can get the hell out of here until Monday. I'm free. I can't wait to go out tonight. I think I'll quit this two-bit job on Monday. The boss can kiss my ass. I've never been to Phoenix. Maybe I'll try my luck there.*

The cycle continued.

George morphed into his other personality, Bennett. He took a long shower and put on his finest suit. He checked himself out in the mirror. *Hey, good looking, head's up, shoulders back, I'm oozing confidence because I'm one lucky son of a bitch. Money is no object.* George lived frugally in a one-room place that had a bed, dresser, closet, and TV. He spent his money on clothes, and having a good time. *To hell with everyone! There are always new people to meet, to go to bed with, to kill...*

"Hi, I'm Bennett. I'd like to buy you a drink if you're interested."

"Sure, you're cute," said Jose.

"Come here often?" asked Bennett.

"A few times but you're new."

"Yeah, I'm not from around here but I decided to check out this place tonight...

"Let's have a few drinks and dance."

"I'd love to."

It came to closing time, 2 a.m. He bought the last round for himself and his new friend. "You know this party doesn't have to end." Bennett hoped Jose would invite him home.

"No?" responded Jose hopefully.

"Well, I don't live near here but if you want, we can take this party over to your place." Bennett was so excited he nearly spilled his drink.

"I'd love to. I just live around the corner."

"Let's go," said Jose. They downed their drinks and headed off.

"Damn it. Number six. This man wasn't a prostitute. In fact, he was a businessman: a pillar of the community. If we don't solve this soon, we're going to be walking a beat in the kiddies' park." Miller looked at Kelby. "Tonight, I want every available detective and off-duty cop; I don't care if you have to pull them off of sick leave, vacation, or whatever else they're doing, to go undercover in every bar, nightclub, and dance place in the surrounding area. Dr. Delmonico believes whoever it is will be out again tonight. Someone had to have seen something," said Miller.

The wire lit up. Delmonico was right. There had been unsolved murders in San Diego, San Francisco, and Las Vegas that fit the pattern: six, five, and seven to be exact.

"It looked like he moved a lot," remarked Kelby.

"We have to catch him tonight before he decides to leave town," said Miller.

Saturday night is the loneliest night of the week. Oh yeah, for some people, but not for me. Yeah, baby, yeah. I'm going out and having some f-u-n. Fun! I heard Aladdin's is exciting. Yeah... Aladdin's. That's where I'm going tonight. This fellow is off to get some action.

"Now everyone get this through your heads. He's going to be out there tonight," said Miller. "We don't have a clue what he looks like but we're looking for a guy who lights a room, with his presence, is narcissistic, charming, charismatic, and probably spends lots of money on drinks. He's a good dancer and he talks to women as well as men. He likes everybody. He kills everybody. We've got six dead bodies in the morgue each one with a 6" knife wound in their back and semen on the spot where he stabs them to confirm that. He may be carrying a small bag or the knife is in his pocket. We checked knives shops in the area and came up empty but he could have bought them at hunting shows or sporting goods stores so that doesn't mean anything. He ties up his victims but in two of the murders, he used his tie, not rope. He gags them too. He's evolving. Take nothing for granted. You see something, you call it in. We'll probably be hauling in innocent people tonight but we don't have a choice. Go with your gut. If someone doesn't look right, move in. Got it?" said Miller.

All the detectives addressed by Miller nodded in agreement.

"Your name is...?" Bennett squealed with excitement.

"Francine."

"Francine? Pretty name. I'm Bennett. Can I buy you a drink?"

"Yes, that would be great."

"Waitress." Bennett motioned to her to come over.

"Yes?" as she laid napkins down in front of Bennett and Francine.

"I'll have a Screwdriver."

"And you, Miss?"

"I'll have a Manhattan"

"So you drink Screwdrivers. Is that a subliminal suggestion?" Francine looked at Bennett and laughed.

"Maybe... but I like vodka. Are you from Manhattan?" asked Bennett.

"No, but I am from New York. Ever been?" She blinked her eyes and tilted her head.

"No, but I'd like to go someday. Let's dance," said Bennett as he took Francine's hand and led her to the dance floor.

Miller and Kelby entered Aladdin's and checked out the bar and dance floor and they immediately picked

up on Bennett. They watched intensely as he danced
with the young Asian lady. He was quite the showman
on the floor. They went back to their table to drink
their drinks and stayed a couple the whole evening
and as the bar started to empty at 2 a.m., she asked
him home. The detectives followed them out to her
place. They had no evidence yet that he was the one.
They were another couple making a connection on a
Saturday night. It was the 70s… Bar hopping, discos,
dancing, free love, murder…

Miller and Kelby stared through the window of
Francine's apartment from a distance using binoculars
while she offered Bennett a drink. They watched
intensely while he drank his drink and she started to
undress. He finished his drink and dropped his clothes
on the floor and then he made passionate love to her.

"You know, I feel like we're a couple of perverts."

"Well, there are ten other teams, peeking in ten
other windows, so if we're perverts, they must be
too."

"But if he's our guy, then we aren't, right?"

"Right!"

"What a stinking way to spend a Saturday night."

Miller and Kelby believed they had their man.
They continued to watch as Bennett and Francine
finished making love. She rolled over on her side to
go to sleep. He rolled over in the other direction and
went for his necktie, rope, and the knife he kept in
his coat pocket. He stuffed the tie in her mouth and

began to tie her hands behind her back when the detectives busted in through the window. Kelby held him down while Miller disarmed him.

Bennett screamed, "What are you doing? I didn't do anything wrong."

"What's your name?" said Miller.

The Bennett personality was gone and George took his place. "My name is George… George Watkins. I don't know what I'm doing here. Who is this woman? Why am I in her bed? I have no clothes on. Please, please let me get dressed. I didn't do anything wrong."

"Just like Delmonico said." Kelby shook his head.

The detectives looked at the woman while they untied her. "You're a very lucky young lady. You were almost his seventh victim," said Miller.

───────────

Previously published by Maudlin House

The Alphabet Murders

Joe Miller and Bill Kelby of the Major Case Squad showed up on the scene of a possible homicide after they were told there was a dead body in the Penthouse Suite of the Diamond Hotel located on 6th and Broadway. Downtown had some expensive places to stay but it wasn't far from Skid Row and the riff-raff that existed there. Could the two be related?

"So, who found the body?" Miller asked the officers on scene.

"The maid did when she brought fresh towels up to the room as requested over the phone," replied one of the officers.

"Well, *he* didn't request them," replied Kelby sarcastically as he inspected the body. "He's been dead for more than two hours. Rigor has already set in."

"Who called?" asked Miller to the Housekeeping Manager.

"A woman; we didn't ask her name. She said she needed a set of towels sent up so… we sent them up."

"Are you sure it was a woman?" asked Miller.

"Yeah, I guess," the housekeeping manager said.

"How many people were registered to the room?" Kelby asked the Front Desk Manager.

"One… a businessman… named Bob Dirken," replied the Front Desk Manager.

"So, Mr. Dirken had some company tonight." Miller started to pace and turned to the other detectives and said, "Okay everybody, can anyone tell me how he died? Come on… a little speculation here. No knife, no gun, he wasn't strangled. Overdose? Doubtful. A heart attack? Maybe. Wait… check this out. Looks like Mr. Dirken had a heart condition but his digitalis medication is empty. Maybe someone spiked his drink?" Miller bagged the bottle.

"Maybe this someone was a person who Mr. Dirken wasn't supposed to be with?" said Kelby, speculating as he looked at Miller. "He had company and depending on if he's married, the company left to avoid embarrassment, but… what if the company gave him the overdose of heart medicine before he or she left?"

"What if the company was a professional call girl and he's married? That could create a load of problems. Hey Kelby, remember last week, we had a case where a rich guy was found dead in his office late at night and it was ruled inconclusive due to him ingesting too much digitalis. *He* had a heart condition. Now we have another case of a dead rich guy with a heart problem. Perhaps the two are related. Miller started to pace faster.

"The autopsy showed he recently had sex too. We thought he gave himself his own happy ending but maybe he had a visit from a professional also. He died in a high rise office late at night. No one was in, not even the cleaning crew. The estimated time of death was 11 p.m. but the body wasn't found until 7 the next morning when his secretary came in and saw him sprawled out on the floor, with a bourbon glass nearby." Kelby gave Miller that narrowed-eyed look he gets when he feels fear and said, "Not *another* serial killer."

"The guy with a split personality disorder who killed people he picked up in bars, nightclubs, and discos was more than enough to last me a lifetime," replied Miller. "I see there is only a single bourbon glass."

"So he was a cheap bastard and didn't offer his company a drink."

"Let's not jump to conclusions that the two deaths are related."

"Man, Joe, I hope not. Then what we have is the possibility that a high class call girl is killing her Johns. She has sex with her rich businessmen clientele and then for whatever reason offs them… Real kinky. What happened? They refused to pay? They didn't like their lay?"

"Who knows? We need to wait for the autopsy and see what the coroner says. In the meantime, let's see the department psychologist to get perspective on this."

Seeing the commotion, a well-dressed sophisticated woman walked over to the bar and motioned the bartender to come over. "So, what's going on," asked the lady, whose name was Sheila.

"Oh, some guy died in one of the suites upstairs."

"Oh, how awful," she said as left the bar. She walked down 6th Street and hailed a cab. A big smile crossed her face. *That's another one I got away with. The dirty bastard! The first one was in his office and he wanted to cheat me out of my fee. They're all alike. They can all die as far as I am concerned. I need to go to my book and kill them all. They used me and didn't care. Now, I'm going to use them, take them for as much money as I can, and kill them. How perfectly wonderful.*

"So Joe, Bill, what can I do for you tonight?… You didn't get me out of bed to stare at me." Dr. Delmonico yawned.

"Well, Doc, we have a big problem. We think a woman, most likely a high-class call girl, was at the scene of rich businessman's death. The only thing we know definitely was a lady called housekeeping for towels and when the maid came up, she was gone, and the man in the bed was dead," said Miller.

"Interesting."

"What is?" replied Kelby.

"She could have left without anyone knowing she was there, yet she called housekeeping. She wanted him to be found on her time table. I assume you dusted for prints, right?" Dr. Delmonico raised his right eyebrow waiting for an answer.

"Yeah, and there weren't any." Miller pursed his lips.

"Most likely she wore gloves and/or wiped the place down. She could have called from either a house phone or a pay phone." Dr. Delmonico poured himself a glass of water. He turned around to face them waiting for the next question.

"We should get a printout on the hotel phones, right?" replied Kelby.

"It would be a waste of time. You'll find she more than likely used a pay phone outside the hotel... So you're sure it's a woman?" asked Dr. Delmonico in a concerned voice.

"Uh, not a 100% sure but housekeeping said it sounded like a woman. That's all we have to go on... We have another case that might be linked to this one. We thought that it was a natural death but maybe it's not. What do you think, Doc? You think it's possible we have a high class prostitute offing her Johns?" Miller was hoping for one answer but expecting another.

"I think what we have is a person who is suffering from A.C.E.: Adverse Childhood Experiences. Something in her background like mistreatment by a family member, alcoholism, drug abuse, a family member who was incarcerated, maybe a relative with mental health issues, or a suicide in the family, pushed her to leave home at an early age. Sixty-four percent of people have experienced one A.C.E. growing up and seventeen percent experienced four or more. I suspect your lady probably came from a house where she experienced more than one. Maybe she had an alcoholic parent; and her mother could have been a prostitute, or had mental illness. If your suspect turns out to be a professional call girl, she probably has been on the streets working as a lady of the evening for a long time. It beat the physical, emotional, or mental trauma of living at home. The poor kid only had one way to make a living and that was hooking. It was better to be on the streets than be at home with her family."

"But why now? Why kill men who made her a living all these years?" Kelby kicked the table.

"Something set her off. A.C.E. victims act out in different ways. She probably worked her way up to being a high-class prostitute without a pimp and developed her own cliental of rich businessmen. What set her off you asked? It could be one of them didn't pay for services rendered or a client tried to cheat her on what was agreed upon. Something snapped and now she's killing her Johns," said Dr. Delmonico.

"We don't know how the Johns even died yet. We're waiting for the autopsy on the second victim but our first victim overdosed on digitalis. We believe the second death was the same," said Miller.

"You know that all the Johns won't be on that med. As time goes on, she will be forced to use something else," responded Dr. Delmonico. "This person sounds too smart for a common poison. I would check for needle marks. If you get any more dead Johns, check for potassium chloride. It stops the heart and dissipates quickly. And look for needle marks in the mouth and at the hairline."

"The mouth?" replied Kelby with a surprise.

"No one would think to look there."

"Thanks Doc," said Miller and Kelby in unison.

"Well you were right," said the coroner to Miller and Kelby. "He died of an overdose of digitalis. I reviewed the other autopsy but I would have to exhume the body to do more testing to prove it was a homicide. That death was ruled accidental. I suggest I could do that if you need me to as a last resort."

This is wonderfully delicious. I have the cops running around in circles. I kicked off my high heels and poured myself a glass of red wine. Dummies, all of them, especially the men. The nerve of those idiots not paying my fee, saying I wasn't worth it. After all the years they came to me. After everything I've done for them. I was there when their wives and girlfriends weren't and then they toss me aside like an old shoe. I showed them and I'll show the rest of them too. Tomorrow, I'll pick another man I haven't talked to in a while from my little black book. He probably hasn't been laid recently. It'll be old home week at the farm.

"It's almost morning. Let's knock off and get some sleep, eh?" Miller said to Kelby as he got up from his chair to go home.

"There's something bothering me."

"Like what?'" Miller raised an eyebrow.

"Like the two dead men. The first victim's first name started with an A and the second victim's first name started with B. You think it's a coincidence?"

"Maybe... Oh no, you think our perp is killing in alphabetical order?" said Miller.

"That's all we need. If the papers get a hold of this... God, Joe... we don't know that for sure and we don't have her book so don't even think it.

"If that's true, all I can say is shit," replied Miller.

"Hi Charlie," said Sheila coyly on the phone.

"I told you not to call me here," he whispered on the phone.

"Why not? We had some good fun for a while."

"I've given you up."

"Really? Can you honestly say that? Is your wife taking care of *all* your needs?"

"No... I can't say she is," replied Charlie.

"Want to get together?" Shelia's voice was so enticing over the phone.

"When and where?" Charlie could hardly wait.

"How about that little motel on Third where we used to get it on? We had a lot of good times there."

"Meet you at ten o'clock tonight?" said Charlie hardly containing himself.

"Great. It's been a while. My prices went up but I'll make sure you have a real good time."

"No problem. See you then."

"I brought a nice wine for us to share," cooed Shelia as she put the wine and glasses on the bedside table.

"I take meds. I'm not allowed any alcohol." Charlie hadn't been with anyone and began to sweat at the idea of alcohol and being intimate with his old lover.

"Ah… just one glass won't hurt," whispered Shelia.

"Okay but first, let's get it on. I've been looking forward to this all day. Then the wine."

"But of course. I wouldn't have it any other way." Sheila flashed her white teeth smile. She took her robe off and bent over to kiss Charlie passionately knowing it was his last encounter.

"That was nice. Let's have that wine now." Charlie reached out for his glass.

"Let me pour it, love," replied Sheila with a smirk.

"Sorry to get you out of bed at three o'clock in the morning but the guy in #5 was supposed to be out by two and when he didn't leave, I went to see what was up." said the manager of the motel to both Miller and Kelby.

"A.M.?" responded a totally surprised Miller. "Who leaves a room at 2 a.m.?"

"We rent the rooms by the hour," stated the motel clerk.

"Oh sorry – I've never done an hourly rental before," said Miller sarcastically. "So what happened?"

"When he didn't check out, I went to find out why and found he was dead in the bed."

"You didn't touch anything, did you?" asked Kelby.

"No siree… I left everything the way it was and called you people."

Miller and Kelby went to the coroner.

"Cause of death appears to be tetrodotoxin," said the coroner.

"What the hell is that?" shouted Miller.

"It's pufferfish toxin."

"You gotta be shitting me," exclaimed Kelby.

"No, it appeared like your perp put it in his wine."

"I don't believe this." Miller threw his hands up in the air.

"She's getting creative and evolving… Hey, look at this, Miller. His name is Charlie. Well, that solidifies my theory. She's killing in alphabetical order. Wait till the media gets a hold of this," replied Kelby not believing it himself.

"That, partner, might be our ace in the hole. Her next John will start with a D. If we release this information, it could save some poor bastard from a hook-up. But, then again, she could change her modus operandi. I don't know what to do," said Miller.

"I don't think she'll change her ways. She's too methodical. She had a system in how she has picked and killed her Johns. I bet she thinks she can't be caught," replied Kelby.

"So what are we going to do? Contact every rich businessman whose first name begins with the letter D?"

"You must be nuts if you think we're going to that."

"No one will think I'm nuts if both of us stop another murder. The best thing we can do is release it to the media," said Miller.

"ALPHABET KILLER STRIKES AGAIN" was the headline of the morning paper. Sheila grabbed one off the stand and started laughing. *The cops think they know who they're dealing with. Well they don't.*

Shelia went to her upstairs apartment, took off her shoes, and turned on the TV. It was the lead story on the news. *More bullshit about a suspected prostitute killing her Johns. They don't have a clue. I'm just getting started and they can kiss my ass.*

"Hello, David. How are you? It's been a while," said sweet-talking Sheila on the phone to an old John.

"So it has. How have you been?" David replied.

"Great. I've missed you. Want to get together?"

"Love to but I can't tonight. But tomorrow I'm free. Does that work for you?"

"My prices went up but I promise you'll have a real good time."

"I'm sure I will. We always had a good time. You never disappointed me. Where do you want to meet?"

"How about the Hotel Langtree, Downtown?"

"Okay, how about 9 p.m.?" said David wanting to get off the phone as soon as possible.

"9 p.m. it is. See you there."

David Henderson, head of the biggest tuna business in the country, called the police and asked for the detectives handing the Alphabet Killer Case.

"This is Detective Joe Miller."

"I think I know who you are after. I used to see a call girl but stopped when I got married and she called me after a long time and wants to see me," said David.

"What's your first name?"

"David."

"You might be right. Go through with it. Let me write down the details. We'll have the place bugged and cameras wired in the room to watch so we can catch her in the act of trying to kill you. We need to get evidence against her otherwise all we have her on is a prostitution charge. Don't eat or drink anything she gives you. You bring the liquor and the glasses.

Don't let her or the booze out of your sight for one minute," said Miller.

"David, it's so wonderful to see you," Sheila was dressed in David's favorite black dress with high heel shoes and she had her hair swept off her shoulders. She glowed when she entered the room.

"Same here. It has been a long time. You look beautiful."

"Thank you. I brought some bourbon to toast to us."

"I brought chilled Champagne. I remembered it's your favorite."

"How thoughtful."

"I'd much rather get it on with you. It's been so long. I missed you," said David as he started to get undressed.

"I've missed you too. More than you know." Shelia smirked.

They made love while the men on the stakeout watched via the cameras and listened in on the microphones.

"You know, Kelby, we're always on the outside looking in," said Miller.

"Don't remind me," responded Kelby.

They finished.

"Oh my God, I can't believe how good you were. It's been a long time," said David approvingly.

"You were always one of my favorite clients. It's a pity we lost touch. Come on, let's have a drink."

"Get ready. Here she goes," said Kelby.

Shelia got out of bed and put on her silk robe. She went to the champagne bottle, opened it, and poured the bubbly liquid in the two glasses. She reached into her robe and pulled out a packet of white powder and poured it into one of the glasses.

"That's it. Move, move, move," shouted Miller.

Miller and Kelby busted down the door. David grabbed his pants while they attempted to restrain the running Sheila. She tried to flee to the bathroom to toss the glass of liquid down the sink but was caught before she could get there.

"What are you doing? You're nothing but a bunch of fucking peeping Toms."

"Thanks, David," said Miller as he nodded to him.

"Thank you for being right where you said you'd be."

"You're such a bastard, David! All of you men are bastards," screamed Sheila.

"If we're bastards, what does that make you?" asked Kelby.

"I hate all of you. You're all no good sons of bitches," shouted Shelia as she was handcuffed and taken away.

Miller looked at Kelby and said, "I guess that's one woman's opinion."

———————

Previously published by CaféLit

Burn, Baby, Burn

"Joe, Bill, don't get comfortable. In my office, *now*," bellowed John Jackson, their temporary boss. He was brought in from the Arson Squad to brief the Major Case Squad on a string of suspicious fires that had grown in number and intensity across the city.

The fires, started in garbage cans, were attributed to juvenile males who got their kicks by setting the bins on fire. It graduated to fires in carports and garages. The fire department did their due diligence to try and identify how they were set but it came up inconclusive. After a string of those fires, empty warehouses were set ablaze. No rhyme or reason as to where they were as they were always in different parts of town. Miller and Kelby weren't brought in until the last fire had occurred because a night watchman died. Now it was a murder investigation. The first thing to figure out was if all the fires were set by a gang of juveniles, a string of copycats, or was it much more sinister? Does the city have a pyromaniac on their hands? Or was it possible that each fire was separate and unrelated. It was time to consult the department psychologist, Dr. Delmonico.

"Hello Joe, Bill, what can I do for you tonight?" He stifled a yawn as it was after midnight.

"You did hear there have been several fires of unknown origin that were set throughout the city for the past several weeks. It's been in the papers and on radio and TV. Well, it finally made it to the desk of the Major Case Squad because a night watchman was burned to death. No one has a clue how to proceed because we don't know if it was kids who set the fires to get their kicks or someone who first lit small fires first to throw us off from what the real purpose was which were the warehouse fires and possible insurance money," said Miller.

"Or maybe we have a psychopath on our hands. Whoever did those was sloppy. The garbage and garage fires could have been covered up from arson but not the warehouses. Someone dropped lit papers soaked in gasoline around the warehouses: What are we dealing with, Dr. Delmonico? A pyromaniac? Someone who gets their kicks off of watching things burn˙or a bunch of juveniles getting their gang initiation?" said Kelby.

"I hate to say it but I have a bad feeling about this one. My theory is the perpetrator is just one person who lights fires for thrills and attention, or possibly money. May I ask who called them in?" asked Dr. Delmonico.

"A man," said Miller.

"The same man or a different one every time?"

"We haven't checked," responded Kelby.

"You need to get with someone that can do a voice print. That's a lead worth pursuing. If it is the same person, he's could be doing it for kicks, and then this person graduated in size and intensity. The fires progressed from garbage bins to garages to warehouses, and the size and risk associated with the fires will increase over time as the fire setter needs more excitement to achieve the same high. That means a bigger fire with each event. If he is a true pyromaniac, which I suspect is the case, he becomes sexually excited watching things burn."

Dr. Delmonico paused because what he was about to say was extremely upsetting. "This type of perpetrator is often voyeuristic and may wait for the fire trucks to show up at the scene; sometimes he calls them in himself and I say 'he' because a high percentage of arsonists are male. Whoever is doing this might have a camera on him so he can photograph his handiwork. He takes pictures of the fires and the spectators at the scene so he can relive the experience again and again. Sometimes, the last person suspected is a first responder, *and* he could even be an off duty firefighter or one on duty one who slips out for a bit to set the fire and then is back for the call. Then he can be a hero in attendance."

"But what about the night watchman that died?" asked Miller.

"I'm sure that was accidental," replied Dr. Delmonico.

"What do we look for?" asked Kelby.

"Before the building fire, I would have said a young male. But now… I'm inclined to think it might be a firefighter, who gets off on setting and watching fires. That's why he fights them. For the thrill! He probably suffers from a variety of other mental problems including a hero's complex. But you aren't going to like what I really think," replied Dr. Delmonico.

"There's more?" said a surprised Miller.

"He holds down a steady job. And if he's a firefighter, he's had an issue about fire since he was a kid."

"How could he be a firefighter? Wouldn't he have an arrest record?" asked Kelby.

"Not necessarily if he was very careful. He probably was never picked up for setting fires. Maybe he set little fires when he was a kid. That's where it started. He could have lived in a rural area and have run with a pack. As he grew up, he decided to get a job in the fire department. I mean that's how you can have your cake and eat it too. Be a fire fighter and enjoy watching things burn."

"What do you think triggered this string of recent fires?" said Miller.

"Hard to say… Maybe it was a death in the family, or a divorce or nothing at all. He just wanted to go back to a time where things were simpler. He reverted back to something that gave him pleasure and comfort and that was setting fires and enjoying the spectacle. Or maybe there isn't any trigger. And if he *is* a firefighter, God help us."

"You don't have any recommendations, do you?"

said Kelby, hoping against hope that Dr. Delmonico had an answer.

"I would start with the roster of firefighters that were off-duty during the time when most of the recent fires occurred."

"The problem is, it isn't in one area. They're all over the city." Miller was so pissed off he kicked the trash can by his desk.

"Sorry, but that is the best I can do for you. But pray you don't have a pyromaniac for hire on your hands. Then, you have the worst of all possible scenarios. He enjoys his work *and* he's being paid for it."

"Joe, what are we going to do? Tell the Captain that Dr. Delmonico thinks one of our Los Angeles' finest is setting the fires," asked Kelby.

"We better have something more than a hunch before saying anything," said Miller.

"Here's a map of the city and it's been marked up with all the suspicious fires in the past six months," said Miller as he tacked up the map on the bulletin board.

"You got to be kidding. There're that many fires?" responded Kelby.

"Yeah, TC stands for trash can with the date next to it. CG stands for carport/garage, and finally WH in a rectangular box stands for warehouse fire."

"Maybe we can draw a circle around them and see which firehouses are in the area."

Miller took a red pencil with a ruler and saw there were four firehouses in the entire area.

"Now we have to narrow down who worked there and review their records. Come on, let's pull them," said Kelby.

"If the Fire Commissioner finds out we're doing this, then we're dog meat," replied Miller.

"Then why did they bring us in if they didn't want us to find out the truth?"

"Sometimes they *say* they want to know but they really don't."

"Lovely."

"I'm right under everyone's nose. Such a laugh watching everyone freak out. I light the fires; the Fire Department, our brave men in blue, yeah right, puts them out but they don't have a freaking clue who is behind it. They're all running around like dogs chasing their tails. I can't believe how incredibly funny that is."

"Between the four firehouses, there were eighty possible full-time employees, plus part-timers, and fill-ins. There were a handful of temporaries and support personnel: totaling over one hundred suspects," stated Miller.

"Well, go on," said Kelby. "Let's start looking at the personnel files."

You might as well brew some fresh coffee. We're gonna be here a while," replied Miller."

Miller and Kelby had been going through the records for four hours when their boss flew through the door screaming, "What in the Sam Hill are you two doing?"

"We're pursuing leads. This is the only place we've looked so far, according to Dr. Delmonico," said Miller.

"But one of our own? Are you nuts?" said their boss John Jackson.

"We have to rule it out… Look, you brought us into this after the death of the night watchman. You didn't have any leads. Let us rule this out and then we'll go in another direction," replied Kelby.

"Fire Commissioner Jones is going to split a gut when he hears this."

"Don't tell him. He doesn't have to know. Only if we find something, okay?" said Miller.

"Because… what if it *is* someone high-up like the Fire Commissioner or a Fire Captain."

"The two of you *are* nuts. I came to tell you; here's another one for your fire board: a warehouse in the garment district. It went up twenty minutes ago. If you hurry, maybe you can put your theory to the test," said Jackson.

Their boss shook his head as Miller and Kelby grabbed their coats and flew out the door on their way to the current fire. The four alarm fire was increased by two more alarms after they got there. They were more interested in the crowd watching the fire than the fire itself so Miller and Kelby split up and made their way through the mob of people. They looked at as many people as they could. There were the looky-loos staring at the fire but nobody fit the arsonist's profile. There were some photojournalists taking pictures for the morning paper. Maybe one of them could be the arsonist? Is it possible they were off-base for focusing on firefighters?

Miller told Kelby they needed to get all the papers covering all the fires and see what the write-ups said and if there was a common thread. They went back to the squad room and started pulling articles. Were the fires covered by one journalist or a bunch of them? If it was one, then they have their suspect and would need to pursue him.

Miller and Kelby spent the night combing through the stacks of newspapers and came up empty.

"I think we should go home, get some rest, and start again tomorrow," said Miller.

"Another delicious fire. Ahhh… Burn baby burn," I whispered under my breath. "Now I'll go back to my office and wait for the report of the fire to cross my desk. They'll never figure out that the State Fire Commissioner is behind all these fires. Dumbbells. They can go chase their tails. Soon I will have all the money I need."

The next morning, Miller and Kelby continued going through the fire station's personnel records but both got the feeling it was someone higher up the food chain.

"I'd bet two weeks' pay it's a Captain or someone in the Commissioner's office," said Miller.

"I wouldn't take the bet because I feel the same way. Maybe someone knows something but is keeping quiet for fear of losing their job," replied Kelby.

"No, I think it's more involved than that. I think the guy works alone. He comes and goes as he pleases and looks like he's inspecting the scenes of the fires or at least reviewing detailed reports and knows exactly what we know. He's not stopping but he's being cautious. No one could tell this guy anything because he knows everything. Now, who's in such a position?" asked Miller.

"Well, the County Fire Commissioner, the City Fire Commissioner, and the State Fire Commissioner. They are the three top people who would know everything about every fire in the area."

"Then I think we need to concentrate our efforts on those three people. If we come up empty, then we'll go back and look at the four stations. By the way, where do these Commissioners work and live? Are *they* in the fire zone?"

"Let me check... Well, the State Commissioner and the City Commissioner live within the fire area."

"Then I think they're our two primary suspects," said Miller.

"And what if we're wrong? Huh, Joe, what if?

We're the ones whose asses will get chewed off if both of them are innocent." He went over to his partner and looked him in the face. "What are we going to do?"

"Our job, partner. Nothing ventured, nothing gained. We have to sniff around. It wouldn't be the first time we lost our ass," said Miller.

"Hey, you two, there's another fire at 4th and Pacific. Get a move on," yelled John Jackson.

Miller and Kelby ran out of the squad room with pictures of their suspects. One or both would probably be at the fire but tying either of them to being the arsonist would be something else.

Miller and Kelby arrived at the scene. It was fully engulfed and instead of watching the fire like everyone else was, they were looking at faces in the crowd. In the back, they saw the State Fire Commissioner. Their hunch was right but that alone was no basis to arrest him. They needed evidence. Miller and Kelby followed him back to his black station wagon. Miller pulled out his camera as he stood in the shadows and discretely snapped pictures of him as he sat there watching the fire with a big smile on his face. There had to be a way to get a search warrant. Captain Jackson wasn't going to be pleased.

"That was a fantastic fire… And I made 50K in cash for setting it. I can't believe how much I enjoy this job. The joy I

45

receive from starting fires and being paid for it. Wonderful! I have almost a million bucks in a tax-free account in Geneva. It's time to split this town and enjoy my life. I am fifty years old. I have a lot of living to do. Only one more job and I resign from my job as Commissioner and I'm off to Switzerland for the rest of my life. The money is there and with money come women and the good life. Just one more fire. That's all I need to do. It will be my coup de grace. Burn, baby, burn."

"On this alone, I can't issue a search warrant. It's all circumstantial. Stake him out and hope that he makes a mistake," said Captain Jackson.

Miller and Kelby went back to their desks to prepare to stake out the State Fire Commissioner's house, 24/7, until he made a mistake. They worked out a schedule with another pair of detectives: Twelve on and Twelve off, with Miller and Kelby taking the first shift 9 p.m. to 9 a.m. What did Dr. Delmonico say? The worst of all possible scenarios is a pyromaniac who gets paid?

Three days into the stake out, the suspect left at 9 p.m. Miller and Kelby followed at a discreet distance back to the warehouse district. Kelby had the camera out and shot multiple pictures of the suspect. Miller shut the lights off as he rolled their sedan closer and they followed him to the pier. The State Fire Commissioner got out of his station wagon carrying a can of gasoline and a bunch of newspapers. Kelby got some beautiful telephoto close-ups of him going into the warehouse and coming out. Minutes later, he came out and drove off. The warehouse went up in flames. Miller picked up the microphone and called the fire in. The Commissioner drove around the corner. He kept his lights off, until the news crews and firefighters pulled up to put the fire out.

Miller turned the sedan around and headed back to the station. He got the photos developed and there was enough evidence to issue a warrant.

"This is one warrant I'm going to enjoy serving," said Miller to Kelby.

"Me too. He took one too many bites of the apple."

The State Fire Commissioner went home, showered, changed, and went to a party at the Lt. Governor's house.

Miller pointed to him leaving and the two of them followed him to the house of the Lt. Governor.

"You can have the honor of knocking," said Miller to Kelby.

Knock Knock.

The butler came to the door. "Yes, may I help you?"

"We're here to see the State Fire Commissioner," replied Miller.

They waited at the door until he came to see who wanted him.

"Yes, what do you want?" said the State Fire Commissioner.

"We have a warrant for your arrest for arson. You have the right to remain silent,…" said Miller.

"This is an outrage… there must be some mistake," he shouted. "You must be crazy if you think you can arrest me."

"No mistake, sir," said Kelby.

"I'll have your jobs for this," he screamed.

"I don't think so, sir. We have you on film starting tonight's warehouse fire," said Miller.

He dropped to his knees while the police were handcuffing him. "NO… NO… NO… this can't be happening. I had it all planned."

Miller looked at Kelby. "You know what they say about plans."

"No… what?" said Kelby.

"The best-laid plans of mice and men often go awry adapted from a line in *To a Mouse*, by Robert Burns. His exact words are 'No matter how carefully a project is planned, something may still go wrong with it,' " stated Miller.

"I guess he didn't read Burns…" replied Kelby.

"His loss," said Miller.

Previously published by CaféLit

The Nursing Home Murders

"Joe, Bill, step into my office for a minute and close the door," said their boss Captain Andrew Reno of the Major Case Squad.

Miller and Kelby went into Captain Reno's office not knowing that this murder case would be one of their toughest cases of their five years together.

"Have a seat," offered Captain Reno.

"What's up?" asked Miller.

"What I am about to tell you is not to go any further than this room until we can come up with some suspects and I mean hard core information that will convict whoever is doing this."

"Doing what?" asked Kelby.

"Killing elderly people in nursing homes," Reno said.

"What?" replied Miller.

"Yeah, you heard me. Someone or multiple people are killing elderly people in nursing homes. We had four deaths in the last week alone. The medical examiner thought at least three of them were suspicious but he is checking into all four."

"How do you know the people weren't... you know... ready to kick off and their deaths are a coincidence?" questioned Miller.

"We wouldn't have known except one of the victims was my aunt," said Captain Reno.

"Your *aunt*?" said Kelby.

"Yes. She went into the nursing home to recover from hip surgery. She was supposed to come home in a week. My uncle arranged for home care and then the place called and said she was dead."

"And you did an autopsy?" asked Miller.

"Of course. It was inconclusive but there are many substances that can be given that won't leave a trace. You know that."

"Yeah, potassium chloride is one. Stops the heart and isn't traceable," stated Kelby.

"Maybe it's a fluke," said Miller.

"No way. My aunt was as strong as an ox. My uncle is devastated. It shouldn't have happened. We're still running a tox screen for other possible substances in her blood. I'm telling you, something's wrong. The week she died, there were three other deaths. It can't be a coincidence."

"You think we have an Angel of Death floating around?" asked Kelby.

"That's what you two are going to find out. One of you will have to go undercover while the other snoops around the home. No one knows you so that's a plus. Since my aunt was well known, most of the guys here went to see her, you know, and dropped off flowers and candy. You were trailing that arsonist and weren't around when my aunt was sick so you two are the perfect cover."

"Man, I hate hospitals. Do we *have to* investigate from the inside?" said Miller.

"Yes, because one of you is going in with a broken leg and will be unable to get around. This is the best way to do this because all four of the victims were bed-ridden."

"But aren't we a little young to be in a nursing home," asked Kelby.

"No. Actually, I have someone coming in to put some grey in your hair, Joe."

"Seriously?" said Miller.

"Yes, we're going to make you about fifteen years older and you're gonna have a couple of health conditions in addition to the broken leg."

"Terrific."

"Bill, you have to be there day and night. You'll be Joe's back-up. They have to think that you and Joe are brothers and are from a tight knit family."

"I'm not going there until I talk to Dr. Delmonico. I want to know what we're walking into," said Miller.

"Good Afternoon, Joe… Bill, so what are you working on today that can I help you with?"

"I'm going undercover in a nursing home and I'm kind of concerned because I'm going to be physically laid-up," replied Joe Miller.

"In what way?" asked Dr. Delmonico.

"One leg is gonna be in a cast."

"Do you have to be a patient in a nursing home to get the needed information?" asked Dr. Delmonico.

"Someone or maybe more than one person is

knocking off old people. There were four deaths last week alone in this place and we can't rule out foul play. So what are we up against?" asked Kelby.

"Well… there are at least four motives I can come up with," began Dr. Delmonico. "First, your suspect could be doing it for altruistic reasons; he kills but gets no reward out of it. Or, there's the opposite reason: your suspect kills for selfish purposes. The people he cares for are a bother to him so by killing them, he saves time and effort. The third reason is for revenge. Maybe he took care of a friend or family member and he hated doing that. Care giving is a thankless task and perhaps he was treated poorly by that person so he's taking his hatred out on others. Finally, without knowing your case, the killings could be racially motivated."

"We can rule out the last one because the four who died were different sexes and races," replied Miller.

"Then you're looking at the first three. Whatever the reason, he wanted these people dead and went to at great lengths to achieve his goal. Be careful."

"You can bet on that," said Miller with Kelby nodding in agreement."

"Man, I hate my job," exclaimed John, the night shift orderly.

"I do too," replied Ed, the other orderly sitting across from him.

"If *you* hate it so much, why don't you go look for something else?"

"What? Wiping people's butts is all I know. I took care of my father and now this. Jesus, I just wish I had been afforded the opportunity to go to college like my brother. You don't see *him* doing this."

"Yeah, but at least, it's a living."

"Yeah, maybe it's a living but not much more than that. I can't keep doing this the rest of my life. These people aren't living; they're existing. What I'm doing is providing a service. I'm easing them out of life painlessly. Some of these people have been here months, others, for only a few days. It's time to empty the place of the dead wood," exclaimed Ed.

I don't like it," said Bill.

"*You* don't like it. I'm the one that gets to have his leg in a cast and pee in a bottle. You better be around to catch this son of a bitch," said Miller.

"Let's not assume it's a man. It could be a woman."

"Okay… bitch or son of a bitch. It's up to you to find him and you better do it quickly before I'm next on the menu."

"I want my brother to have the best care," said Kelby.

"Yes, Mr. Kelby. He won't be here too long. Just long enough for him to get back on his feet from the accident," said Hospital Social Worker Jack Patterson.

"Joe, did you hear that? You won't have to stay too long. You'll have physical therapy and you'll be out of here in no time." He wheeled Miller into his room.

"Here's your room," said Mr. Patterson.

"Hi, I'm your roommate," yelled Mr. Hamilton.

"This is Mr. Hamilton. He's a little hard of hearing but he's here to rehab from his heart surgery."

Miller rolled his eyes. *Oh dear God, Help me.* "Terrific…" he whispered to Bill. "You better get me the hell out of here."

"Patience… Patience…" said Kelby to Miller quietly.

"Well, Mr. Kelby, visiting hours have come to an end."

"Thank you Mr. Patterson. I'll be back to visit my brother tomorrow."

Patterson left and Kelby bent down and whispered in Miller's ear, "You got your .22?"

"In the holster attached to the upper part of my casted leg. I wouldn't leave home without it."

The 11 p.m.-7 a.m. shift came on and so did the Angel of Death. There was an eerie quiet and then the sound of a cart going down the hall, stopping abruptly at Mr. Hamilton's bed.

"Here you go, Mr. Hamilton. It's time for your medication, something for you to sleep."

"Don't take it," screamed Miller as he grabbed his .22 and faced it toward his roommate's bed.

"Alright, freeze right there," said Kelby as he flew into the room, his .38 revolver out. He grabbed the hypo in the suspect's hand. Kelby disarmed him and called for back-up.

Miller looked around. "This seemed too neat and clean. There must be another one. We can't resume this cover. We'll have to come up with another way."

"Okay jackass, why *are* you killing old people?" said Miller.

"Why not? They are a drain on society. They lie there in the bed and give nothing back. I'm tired of washing their asses. They are better off dead," said Ed.

"Why you no good son of a bitch!" Kelby started to lunge at the suspect but was held back by Miller.

"Don't you get it? I'm doing *them* a favor *and* lessening the load on myself and society. There will always be one more behind them to fill the bed. I can't get rid of *these people* fast enough."

Kelby let loose and slammed his fist on the table. "You have a partner. We want his name."

"Find him yourself."

"You *want* to take the rap for all the murders?" said Miller.

"Whether it's one or five or ten, it's all the same. You can only execute me once." Ed lit up a cigarette and blew the smoke into the air in ringlets.

"Shit," said Kelby.

"We have to go back in but a different way. This guy

was on the 11 p.m.-7 a.m. shift. Maybe his friend is too, but wasn't working last night. What about one of us going in as an orderly?" said Kelby to Captain Reno.

"Okay, you two figure out who goes in and who will be the back-up."

"I had my hospital duty, Bill. Since it's *your* idea, you go. I'll be your back-up." Miller gave Kelby a big smile as if to say Ha, Ha, you're the goat.

"You have a problem in your hospital, Mr. Williamson. You're the Hospital Director. We suspect another Angel of Death is floating around on your 11 p.m.-7 a.m. shift. I want you to hire me so I can snoop around. If you don't, I'll get a court order and present my investigation to the Nursing Home Commission and shut you down permanently," said Kelby. "It's your choice."

"Since you put it that way, you're hired," replied Mr. Williamson.

"I'm in, Joe."

"Good. I'm your back-up. You got your .38 leg holster gun?" asked Miller.

"Absolutely."

Wearing a wireless microphone, Kelby entered the dark corridors of the nursing home. It was 11:02 p.m. He clocked in and headed for the nurses' station.

"I can hear everything on your wireless mic," said Miller, into Kelby's ear receptor.

"The damn microphone is causing my chest hair to itch," whispered Kelby.

"Put up with it."

Kelby walked into the break room. A surprised John greeted him with suspicion. "Who are you?"

"I'm the replacement on this shift. I got hired this morning."

"Where's Ed?" John looked Kelby up and down. He was still not too sure who he was.

"I have no idea. I answered an ad in the paper, was hired, and told to report here tonight."

"Well come on, I'll show you the ropes. Night shift tends to be slow. The nursing staff gave out the meds. They checked the catheters. We need to turn the patients every two hours so they don't get bed sores. That is, *if* we remember… Ha ha ha ha."

Bastard. Kelby could barely control his feelings.

"There's a lounge I like to hang out at until the nurses come and scream at me… You know, I wish all the patients would die already. Half of them are vegetables. Half are rehabbing but they're the bigger pains in the ass than the vegetables because they constantly ask for something. They remind me of the family members I took care of before I came here. Well, I showed them."

"You did? What did you do?"

"I put them all out of their misery."

"How? I mean you didn't get caught."

"There are ways. Potassium Chloride, Digitalis, Rat Poison, Arsenic. But that was years ago."

"And now?"

"I use pufferfish poison. It works like a charm."

"Pufferfish poison, really?"

"There are plant poisons that work well; Botox is a good one, and there are poisons that are put on the end of the blow darts that come from frogs in South America. Whatever you use, you must be careful how you handle them."

"So when did you use this... this pufferfish poison."

"I used it last week on some woman with a broken hip. She was very demanding. Well, I stopped that."

"Go, Go, Go," screamed Miller into his transmitter.

"You're under arrest for murder." Kelby took a good look at this creep who murdered sick and old people.

"What?" said John.

"And my boss is going to be very happy we caught the person who murdered his aunt."

"Prove it."

Kelby opens his shirt to reveal his wireless microphone. "We just did... With your confession." John attempted to reach out to hit Kelby but Kelby grabbed his arm and cuffed him behind his back. He threw the bastard murderer to his partner.

The coroner found traces of pufferfish poison throughout Captain Reno's aunt's body. The medical examiner now had the ability to go back and exhume the last ten people who died in that place.

"You did well, Joe… Bill. Thank you from my family to both of you," said Captain Reno.

"I feel like I need a good long hot shower after this assignment to wash the filth away," said Kelby.

"Me too," replied Miller.

Previously published in *Otherwise Engaged: A Literature and Arts Journal* Volume 13, June 2024

The Clown Murders

Jason saw an advertisement in the paper that the Grand Clown Convention was being held today and tomorrow at the Convention Center. He planned to attend. He worked part-time for a telegram company dressed as a clown, delivering ridiculous messages to people, while making little cute dogs out of balloons and blowing a big horn. He worked this side job for the past year so he could to qualify for an invitation to the Convention. Jason's motive wasn't one of happiness but one of hate. He'd despised clowns ever since he was a kid.

There will be hell to pay for what that clown did to me at my 5th birthday party. The other children laughed at me because I was so scared of the clown that I peed my pants. That bastard! Everyone thought it was so funny. Well, no one will laugh at me anymore because I'm gonna get revenge on ALL OF THEM! They'll be sorry they ever became clowns. Frightening little children like that. The SOBs – all of them but I'll get 'em… A Clown Convention. It's nothing but a bunch of grown-ups walking around in fright wigs, a big nose and large shoes. It's the perfect place to kill every one of them. I'll be doing the world a service. Ever since the comic books came out, there were clowns. There was the Joker: the nemesis to Batman: an evil clown. I say to hell with all of them: good and bad including Bozo and Hobo Kelly.

The newspaper had the times when the Los Angeles Convention Center opened and closed on

Saturday and Sunday. Hundreds of people dressed as clowns would be there with booths showing off the latest in make-up, wigs, costumes, and big feet. The people who run this make a ton of money selling crappy merchandise. There would be stupid clown booths, where children could take pictures with their favorite bozo. I never realized that there were so many kinds of clowns until I got into the business.

Jason finished applying the grease paint to his face and worked on making big eyes and red cheeks. He put on a big red nose and a red fright wig. But he could have easily worn orange hair with big ears. One clown looked like another and that was the best part. Putting on make-up and hair was the least of his problems. He had a towel around his shoulders to keep him from getting grease paint on his costume which he put on before starting the make-up process. Then he put on his big feet and white gloves. His outfit was complete.

Jason took the bus. The little kids screamed with delight when they saw him. He made balloon animals to keep the children amused but this just enraged him even more because his own childhood was ruined by a clown. He couldn't stand being in that silly costume.

He'd be one of many clowns at the convention. He even picked a fake name which many of the performers did. His name was Ho Ho the Clown. It wasn't registered so there was no way to trace it back to him. Jason called in sick from his regular job. They didn't know that he had a side job of being a clown. It wouldn't have mattered. He was just an office worker; another cog in a wheel of a large corporation. A job he hated. It was upper management that made the money, had the parties, and ordered the entertainment which included clowns. He could have easily been the company's entertainment and they would have never known it was him.

Screw them. Screw them all. Each and every one of them has it coming. They aren't nice people. Clowns are sick human beings, interacting with children pretending to be wonderful by making balloon animals and doing magic. Parents should be punished for letting their kids get close to them. They all need to die which is exactly what I plan to do. I'll get rid of every one of them and I'll be doing the world a service.

Jason carefully planned how to do away with a many clowns as possible. He decided to use poison and drop it in the punch bowl, not a fast-acting kind, but a slow-acting one that many clowns will have drunk before anyone knew it was laced. He ground up the nightshade plant, which was extremely poisonous, into a fine powder. It was the perfect plan.

He walked over to the refreshment area and started to mingle with the other clowns. The central punchbowl was unguarded. *I mean, who would hurt a clown? HA HA HA. I'll show them.* Jason took out the poison and poured it into the bowl. Another clown came by and Jason quickly stirred the pink liquid with the ladle before pretending to take a cup of the poisoned punch. He stood around for a moment and then left.

Two hours later, clowns began to drop like flies all over the place which prompted a call to the Major Case Squad.

Joe Miller and Bill Kelby walked in and stared at the ground. There must have been at least thirty dead clowns and the only things on the floor other than the clowns were paper cups and pink liquid. It appeared they drank something and all there was around was punch.

"Has CSI arrived yet?" asked Miller to the cop in the immediate area.

"Yeah, they were here and they taped off the area," shouted a beat cop.

Clowns that were still conscious were rushed by ambulance to the nearest hospital in an effort to try and save their lives. Twenty were in critical condition.

"What the hell is going on?" asked Kelby firmly.

"Someone hates clowns from what I can see," replied Miller dryly.

"Ya think? But how did he put the poison in the punch if that's what it is."

"Maybe it came from the manufacturer that way?" asked Miller.

"No, because that's a brand of punch on the shelves at the market and no one had reported anyone else dropping dead. I know because my wife buys it," said Kelby.

"Then I think it had to be a definitely attack on clowns," said Miller emphatically.

"But there are *only* clowns here!" said Kelby practically yelling.

"Precisely. *Then* it's a clown killing his own kind," replied Miller.

"I know this has nothing to do with anything and this is sick of me to say this but I can't stop hearing the song, *Send in the Clowns.*"

"You're right, you *are* sick," said Miller shaking his head.

"We need to talk to the department shrink, now," said Kelby.

"Dr. Delmonico, can you help give us some clarity on why someone dressed as a clown would want to kill others people dressed as clowns?" asked Miller.

"Well, basically you have a person who hates himself for being a clown *and/or* hates clowns in general. Maybe had a bad experience as a child. It could be his parents had a birthday party or he went to a party and there was a clown there. He was traumatized badly by one and now has assumed the identity of the one he hates to get back at them."

"What do you recommend?" asked Kelby.

"You're not gonna like it. One, both, or a group of you will have to go undercover at the convention center dressed as clowns while the rest of the detectives watch like hawks to see if you can find the guy doing the poisoning."

"You sure it's a guy?" asked Miller.

"99% sure. I wish you luck."

Damn! I only got 30 or so clowns and a few more that went to the E.R. They may die if they don't identify the poison in time. That leaves at least 150 clowns who got off scot free. Now what? Maybe they will disband the convention and then how will I get the rest of them?

CLOWN CONVENTION WILL GO ON AS SCHEDULED.

MORE SECURITY WILL BE ON HAND TO KEEP EVERYONE SAFE.

So they are going to continue it. Hooray, I get to try again.

"Joe, Bill, step into my office please. This clown thing at the convention center is a mess. We should shut the place down but the hierarchy won't do it. They are proceeding against our advice. That means both of you along with some other detectives will have to go undercover as clowns to see if you can flush out the murderer."

"Dr. Delmonico already suggested this but no offense, Captain, it was bad enough when we went undercover at the nursing home. But this?" said Miller in an unhappy tone.

"Outside is a profiler from the FBI. As you get into your makeup and wardrobe, you will be briefed as to what to look for. I doubt the killer is going to figure the police will dress up as clowns." Reno walked toward the door.

"Dr. Delmonico, what do you think?" said Miller.

"You look great."

"That wasn't what Miller meant," replied Kelby.

"No, you're playing the part perfectly. Captain Reno is right that the person doing this is going to watch for plain clothes and uniformed officers not thinking one of the people standing next to him is a cop," said Dr. Delmonico.

"But there are over a hundred clowns," replied Kelby.

"Yeah but only one of them is gonna try and poison the punch bowl again," said Dr. Delmonico.

"You think?" replied Miller.

"Definitely. There are four refreshment stations set up and we will be watching all four. Bill, Joe, and two other detectives will be hanging around each station watching for suspicious activity," said Captain Reno.

"He's gotta be a moron to try the same thing again," replied Kelby.

"I didn't say he was smart. He's a clown with a vendetta. He's not thinking straight," said Dr. Delmonico.

"And you're *sure* it's a guy?" asked Miller.

"Trust me, that's the one thing you can bank on," replied Dr. Delmonico.

"Testing one, two, three, four, base to Joe… acknowledge," said Captain Reno.

"I'm here."

"Bill, come in," said Reno.

"Yeah, I'm here, and this damn receiver is itching my chest hair AGAIN," said Kelby.

"Next time, we'll shave you." Captain Reno made the buzzing sound of an electric razor.

"Hey Mister, why are you talking to yourself?" asked a little boy watching Kelby.

"Get away, kid, you bother me."

"Bill, what's going on?" asked Reno.

"Some little kid came up to me and asked why I was talking to myself."

"Is he gone?" Captain Reno's voice cracked with concern as he responded to Kelby.

"Yes."

"Richard, come in," said Captain Reno.

"Yes, I'm here."

"Bob, report."

"Everything is normal," replied Bob.

"Great, any of you see anything suspicious, you yell, signing off for now," said Reno.

Look at the idiots roaming around the convention center and having no clue who the murderer is. Ha! I'll show them. I'll poison the main punch bowl in the kitchen. I secured a pass to get past security. Doing this will be a piece of cake.

"I don't like it," said Kelby. "What if the suspect tried to insert the poison another way?"

"Like what?" replied Miller.

"I don't know but if I were him and saw the police around and I wanted to carry out my plan, I wouldn't do it plain view."

"So what do you think?" said Miller.

"The delivery truck or the kitchen would be two logical choices," replied Kelby.

"Go... Go... Go..." said Miller.

The plain clothes detectives sealed off the back alley. Miller and Kelby opened the door, guns in hand. They entered the kitchen area, and there was Jason putting nightshade in the punch syrup.

"Freeze," said Miller, his gun raised.

Jason pulled a knife, turned quickly, and attempted to throw it at Miller when Kelby shot him in the chest. He dropped the knife as he went down.

Miller bent down and asked, "Why did you want all the clowns dead?"

"Clowns are despicable mean human beings that prey on small children. They are all evil and they needed to be stopped. I'm sorry you stopped me before I finished my mission." With that Jason died.

Miller looked at Kelby and said, "He was a very unhappy sick person."

"Dr. Delmonico was right again. He was traumatized as a kid," replied Kelby.

Miller arose, looked at his partner, and said, "Thanks, Bill, I didn't see the knife."

"You're welcome."

Bill took off his red nose and threw it on the floor along with the orange fright wig. He was totally disgusted. "Let's get out of these outfits."

"I can tell you one thing. I'll never look at a clown ever again and think happy thoughts," said Miller.

"Me neither."

The Rich Man Murder

It was after 10 p.m. when Ed Sherwin decided to drop in on his general contractor, John Shears, at his downtown office. The building was empty. It was so late that even the cleaning crew had been there and left.

"I'm tired of being milked by you," Sherwin shouted to Shears in his angry southern drawl voice. "I've financed three shopping centers and now this… this monstrosity that you fittingly named after me because you wanted more money. What do you think I'm made of?… You think I'm your own personal bank to make withdrawals from? What did you squander that last $500,000 on? Huh?… Boy… I'm talking to you."

Shears didn't like his tone of voice especially being called "boy" by this country bumpkin.

"Well, I'm through… do you hear? Through! I'm not funding your project anymore. Get someone else to be your pigeon."

"Wait, you signed a contract," replied Shears in his proper British tone of voice. "Besides, there were unintentional overruns. The project had unforeseen add-ons. Your wife knew about them." He grabbed the file on his desk, he showed Sherwin the papers and said, "See, she signed the additional contract."

"Well, she didn't have the authorization to do so," Sherwin retorted.

"As your spouse, she does."

"Oh no, she doesn't. Not according to the pre-nup I had drawn up or maybe you didn't refer to that little piece of paper when you asked her to sign the additional agreement. My lawyer will be in contact with your lawyer. We're through. I'm done! Finished! And you can kiss this project good-bye."

Ed Sherwin turned his back and as he reached out to grab the door knob to leave, John Shears yelled, "NO!" Sherwin never made it that far. With a white hot anger he never experienced before, John Shears picked up the statue on his desk and shouted, "I won't let you ruin me!" as he hit Ed Sherwin on the back of the head three times.

Sherwin fell to the floor, dead. Shears looked at him and the statue. Now he had to get rid of the body. He wiped the small amount of blood from the statue on the Persian rug by the dead body, took the rug, rolled Sherwin up in it, dragged him down to freight elevator, and dumped his body into the trunk of Sherwin's own car. There was more than enough room; he drove a 1978 White Cadillac two-door Eldorado. "That trunk could hold two bodies at least," said Shears out loud.

Now, what should I do with the body? Where can I bury him without anyone finding it? I need to show he left town and also show that he had never come to the office to see me... Meanwhile, I'll take him to my ranch and hide him in the gardening shed until I can come up with a suitable place to bury him. It must be a place where no one will ever find the body.

71

Shears got to his ranch, wrapped the body of Ed Sherwin in plastic and placed it in an upright position in the gardening shed. Then he burned the carpet from his office, got back in Sherwin's car, and drove it to the long-term lot at the airport. He bought a one way ticket to Tennessee though a travel agency, found a pan handler at the airport, and paid him to get him on the flight posing at Ed Sherwin. The homeless person fit the general description of Sherwin and the airline wasn't checking IDs on a night flight. Shears gave the man $1,000 and told him to stay the night in Tennessee but take the next plane back under his own name. Shears paid for the one-way ticket back.

Shears took a cab back to his office, picked up his car, and went home.

Three days passed.

I haven't heard anything about Sherwin being missing and as far as I am concerned, no news is good news. So what do I do permanently with the body? I can leave the body where it is a little longer. It's wrapped in plastic and it's cool weather but eventually I have to dispose of it. The shed is located far from any place on the property and no one has a reason to look in it. Think… Think… where can I bury the body???

"Excuse me, is this the Major Case Squad?" said a shorter older red-headed woman standing next to a younger taller voluptuous blonde one.

"Yes, I'm Joe Miller and this is my partner Bill Kelby. What can we help you with?"

"My ex-husband which is her current husband is missing," said the red-head.

"How do you know he's missing?" questioned Miller.

"It's been three days and no one has heard from him and that's not like him," said the blonde.

"Maybe he doesn't want to be heard from. Perhaps he took a vacation," replied Kelby.

"He never leaves without calling me. He might be my ex but we're close friends," said the red-head.

"*And* he didn't pack a suitcase," said the blonde.

"Maybe he had business somewhere and went on a short trip and didn't need any clothes," stated Miller.

"But his car is gone," said the red-head.

"Maybe he drove?" asked Kelby.

"Ed doesn't drive long distances, even though he has a nice car: he has eye problems. He only drives at night if it's urgent. Can't you please check into it?" asked the red-head.

"We're not missing persons," stated Miller.

"We understand that but he has been gone more than seventy-two hours. We we're told that if he met with foul play, you could help," replied the blonde.

"Who told you that?" asked Miller.

"Missing persons," stated the blonde.

"It figures," said Kelby. "Okay, you see that officer over there." Kelby pointed at the other side of the room. "Give him as much information as you can: his full name, any distinguishing features like tattoos, birthmarks, and a current photograph. We'll talk to our Captain to see if we can take the case."

"Thank you," they both said.

"Excuse me, Mr. Shears, we're leaving early tomorrow morning on our trip. You sure you don't want to go with us to Calico Ghost Town,[1]" said Mr. Shears' secretary.

"What?" Shears replied.

"You remember. We're leaving on that trip that the office is taking. We're going to Calico Ghost Town for the weekend. It should be a fun time for all. Some of us are going to camp there and the rest of us are staying in their lodge."

"No, thank you. Maybe some other time," Shears said.

The wheels started spinning in Shears' head.

I found the perfect spot to leave a body: what better place than a ghost town. Why the hell not. I'd have to sneak in and out of the park and if it didn't work out, I could leave the body in the desert and it wouldn't be traced back to me. What a perfect plan.

---

[1] Calico Ghost Town is an actual place that exists as part of San Bernardino Regional Park in the high desert North of Los Angeles. It is open every day but Christmas. There is the mystery house tour, a train ride, and gold panning, among other things to do there, plus gift stores and eating places. They have places to stay or you can camp.

I'm so excited. I went to a payphone to call Calico to make sure the information I heard was correct. Calico is open every day 9-5, closed Christmas Day. Perfect. I'll drive up after they close Sunday night and dump the body in the mine entrance. There won't be much left of it when or if they find him. Maybe some desert animal will make a meal of him. HA. And the best part about it is they'll never trace it back to me. How wonderful!

"Hey Kelby, I just received word that airport police found Sherwin's car in the long-term parking lot at the airport. The boys are going over it now but it looks like it's been wiped clean of prints."

"Not even the dead man's are there?" said Kelby.

"Nope, nothing. This case is looking more and more like this missing man met with foul play. Let's get out to the scene and see if we can find any clues," replied Miller.

Miller and Kelby got to the airport just before the tow truck driver jacked the car up to take it away.

"Excuse me, would you stop for a minute? I'm Detective Bill Kelby and this is my partner, Detective Miller from the Major Case Squad." They pulled their IDs out to show the truck driver.

"Okay, holler when you're finished," the tow truck driver said.

Miller opened the driver's door. "The car is clean like it had been detailed except look at this on the floor, Bill... it looks like it is some kind dirt or

75

manure. Maybe the victim had stepped in something before coming to the airport," said Miller.

Miller took his hanky and picked it up and smelled it before he exclaimed, "It is manure! Someone stepped in it and tracked it into a newly detailed car. Seriously, something definitely ain't right. A spotless car except for that. I don't buy the victim got into his detailed car and then didn't wipe his feet? No way." Miller shook his head.

"Maybe it's from the killer's shoes?" responded Kelby. "I gotta bad feeling that Mr. Sherwin is dead."

"Since his car is here, it could be he went somewhere," said Miller.

"Let's check it out," replied Kelby.

The detectives went to the various airlines and ticket agents and found where a ticket was purchased matching somewhat of a description of Mr. Sherwin. "The records said he bought a ticket to Memphis, TN. And he had no luggage," said the ticket agent.

"One way... Hum... that doesn't make any sense," said Miller.

Kelby asked the ticket agent, "Are you sure this was the man that boarded the plane?" They pulled out a picture of Ed Sherwin. "Look closely."

The ticket agent looked at the picture for a long time and then said, "No, this guy wasn't dressed up. In fact, he wore dirty clothes and smelled bad."

"Thank you," said Miller.

"So now we have someone who posed as the missing guy who took a trip to Tennessee with no return flight. I think someone paid this guy to pose as Ed Sherwin and make it look like he left town on business. What do you think?" asked Miller.

"Sounds plausible," replied Kelby.

"We need to speak to the first Mrs. Sherwin."

Ring, Ring. "Hello, Is this Mrs. Sherwin? This is Detective Miller. I need to ask you a question. Does your husband know anyone in Tennessee?... No? We have a lead that he boarded a plane on a one way ticket there. Okay thanks."

"We need to backtrack and assume that he never left Los Angeles. This looks like a false trail. We need to start with the manure left in the car and find out the last place he went to before he was supposed to have gone to Tennessee," responded Kelby.

"I'll call the second Mrs. Sherwin and ask if she knew where her husband went the night he didn't come home... So, tell me where did your husband say he was going before he didn't come home?" said Kelby.

"He said he was going to talk to Mr. Shears. He's the developer who is building the shopping center Ed's financing," replied the second Mrs. Sherwin.

"Can you give me Mr. Shears address and phone number?" asked Miller.

Miller and Kelby paid Mr. Shears a visit at his office.

"Mr. Shears, we were wondering if you heard from Mr. Sherwin. He hasn't called home in several days and his wife and ex-wife are worried," asked Miller.

"I saw him a couple weeks ago. We discussed business and then he left. I'm sorry I can't help you more gentlemen. You made a ride out here for nothing," replied Shears.

"Oh, it wasn't for nothing. We have to follow-up on every lead," said Kelby.

Each one looked around the office. "What's that?" asked Miller referring to the model of the new shopping center.

"That's the development Mr. Sherwin invested in."

"Some place," stated Kelby.

"Nice office you have here with lots of statues and fine rugs. Looks like a rug is missing," said Miller.

"It's out being clean… Look gentlemen, if you are done, I have work to do."

"Yeah, sure," said Kelby.

Out in the hall, Kelby said to Miller, "Hey Joe, did you notice his shoes had dirt on the sides of it. You think it could be manure?"

"Yeah, I noticed that too. Also the missing rug was definitely long enough to wrap a body up in. We need to stake this guy out. He gives me the creeps," replied Miller.

It was Sunday night. Unbeknownst to Shears, Miller and Kelby had been following him since Friday night. Sunday evening, he drove to his farm in the country. Shears opened the shed and took out a large item wrapped in plastic out and put it in the trunk of his 1979 Mercedes 450SL.

"Let's move in," said Kelby. "And close this case."

"No, let's wait and see where he's gonna take the body. Keep snapping pictures," replied Miller.

Shears drove down the muddy country road on to the highway and went up the Interstate to the high desert.

"Where the hell is he going?" said Kelby.

"I don't know but we have to keep following him!" replied Miller.

After a two hour drive, he got off on Yermo Road and headed to the locked gate of Calico Ghost Town.

"Good thing you filled the gas tank or we'd never have made it this far," said Kelby.

Miller called the Highway Patrol. They were following him with their lights off keeping the light traffic at bay.

He drove to the gate, opened it with a pair of bolt cutters, and drove to the end of the town. Then Shears parked his car at the near the mine entrance. He got out, opened the trunk of his car, and took the body of Ed Sherwin out. He dragged it to the edge of the mine.

Before he was able to push it in, Miller yelled, "Halt, this is the police. Throw out your weapons if you have any and give yourself up."

Shears took out the gun he brought with him and considered making a stand but there were too many of them.

"Don't be stupid Mr. Shears. You're completely surrounded." The town's lights came on plus six police car headlights including Miller and Kelby's.

Shears dropped the gun.

Miller and Kelby went over to put the cuffs on him. Shears had to ask, "How did you know it was me?"

"We didn't at first but your shoes gave you away," replied Miller.

"What, my shoes?"

"Your shoes. You left manure in the dead man's car... a car that had just been detailed and your shoes had some on it too when we went to visit you a few days ago like you had just been to your hiding place. If you had cleaned up after yourself, wiped your shoes, and the floor of the dead man's car, we wouldn't have had any clues to go on as to where you hid the body," replied Kelby.

"I thought you'd find the body where I had stored it so I decided to bury it up here," said Shears.

"You should have buried it on your property," said Miller.

Shaking his head, Shears said, "I can't believe this. I really can't believe this."

"What?" responded Kelby.

"You found me because I had horseshit on my shoes... Damn."

———————————

Previously published by CaféLit

One of Our Novices is Missing

"Hey Joe, you think Shelly came in early and made us a pot of coffee, huh?" said Kelby as they dragged into the squad room from a lack of sleep.

"I certainly hope so. I can use some fresh hot coffee after that mud we drank on the stakeout, but there are three other things I want more: a long hot shower, a large breakfast with eggs, potatoes, bacon, and toast, and a warm bed to sleep in for at least twelve hours," replied Miller.

Overhearing the boys talking, Captain Reno shouted, "Sorry boys, except for coffee and some left over donuts, the sleeping has to wait."

"Aw, come on Captain," whined Miller. "We just got back from three days trailing that murder suspect to the high desert. We haven't even finished the paperwork yet. And you're giving us another assignment?"

"I have no choice. The other teams are out and I have something that came in marked urgent. It's a missing person's case... but before you say that's not your department, it came from the top man himself. You'll have time to go home, shower, and change, but you need to step in my office to be briefed... now!"

Miller and Kelby stopped eating the hard, stale donuts left over from Friday morning and went into Captain Reno's office.

"Mother Superior, I'd like you to meet Detectives Joe Miller and Bill Kelby."

Mother Superior put her hand out to shake each of their hands and they did likewise.

"What can we do for you… Mother?" said Kelby hesitantly.

"One of my novices is missing. Her name is Suzanna Tompkins. She was set to take her final vows Saturday and didn't show up with the rest of the class. I checked the sleeping quarters, chapel, church, and the rest of the grounds but she wasn't anywhere to be found."

"Maybe she got cold feet and went home to her family," replied Kelby.

"Her mother and stepfather were at the ceremony and were as surprised as the rest of us to see she wasn't there. They were there for the ceremony."

"Was *everyone* in the family happy that she was becoming a nun?" asked Miller.

"Her father didn't like it all."

"Did he make his objections known?" asked Kelby.

"Oh, yes. He came to the church Friday morning and asked if Suzanna was still going through with it and then begged her not to. He told her she didn't understand all the ramifications of giving her life to the church. Never marrying, never having children. He wanted her to wait and think about it some more. I understand he spent a great deal of time talking to her.

She had been a postulate and novice for the given amount of time. Of all the women, she was the one most focused on the charitable nature of the church. She loved working with children. She even worked with runaways and helped to reunite them with their families after she got them counseling."

"This lady sounds like she has a big heart. Is there anyone else who could have been against her taking her final vows?" asked Kelby.

"Well, before she came to the church, she was a troubled girl. The church gave her structure. She had been seeing a young man who *said* he was madly in love with her and if he couldn't have her, no one else could," replied Mother Superior.

"So, now we have two suspects: her father and her ex-boyfriend. Anyone else?" asked Miller.

"Not really. You know, some of the girls were jealous but that's normal."

"Mother Superior, you've given us a place to start. Do you have a recent picture of her?" asked Kelby.

"I don't have one in her novice attire but her mother gave me this photo that was taken in her regular clothes when she visited with her on Friday." The Mother Superior pulled out a photo of Suzanna.

"Thank you Mother Superior. Should we have any further questions, leave your phone number with Captain Reno and we'll get back to you if or when we have any information," said Miller.

"Bless you both. I'll be praying you find her soon."

"As I see it there are two possibilities," said Miller.

"And they are?"

"She left willingly or she didn't."

"Brilliant. You thought that up all by yourself."

Ignoring the remark, Miller continued, "If she left on her own volition, then maybe she went to her old boyfriend's place or to her father's house."

"And if not?" inquired Kelby.

"Then we have problems, partner, because it could be foul play and maybe, and I don't want to even think of this as a possibility but she has been kidnapped or even killed."

"Who would want to kidnap a novice nun?" asked Kelby.

"It goes back to the father and the ex-boyfriend to prevent her from taking her final vows. The jealousy with the other nuns has to be checked out but I think that's a dead end," said Miller.

"There could be a third option," stated Kelby.

"Which is?" asked Miller.

"She simply left. She couldn't stand the pressure and needed time to think. So she went somewhere to get her head on straight."

"If that's true, where would she go? I'll drop you off at your home so you can shower, put on clean clothes, and grab some breakfast. Then we'll go over to the church and take a look at her living quarters. We can talk to some of the other novices and nuns. Maybe we'll get lucky, and one of them knows something and hasn't said anything because she doesn't know that she knows," said Miller.

"You want to run that by me again… never mind. I'll see you in ninety minutes," said Kelby.

The detectives arrived at the church after morning prayers had ended. They walked in the back of the building feeling like fish out of water as neither one had been to church since they were children. Kelby attended a Catholic grammar school but that was twenty years ago. He felt a little guilty walking in so he went to the altar, knelt, and crossed himself. Miller stood there waiting patiently for him. Father Johnson approached.

"You must be the detectives that the Mother Superior told me about," he said.

"Yes, Father…" said Kelby. "We're here to see if we can figure out what happened to Suzanna Tompkins."

"Everyone here will give you their utmost cooperation. Where do you want to go first?" Father Johnson asked.

"We'd like to walk around the church grounds, take a look at her room, and see if we can come up with something," said Miller.

"Yes, of course. I'll have one of the sisters show you around."

"Thank you, Father," replied Miller.

Father Johnson walked off and Kelby turned to Miller and said, "I don't have a good feeling about him."

"He seemed nice enough."

"Why? You think he's involved in her disappearance in some way?"

"Yeah, I do... in some way. I just don't know how yet. He seemed like he was purposely detached from the situation."

"I think you're jumping to conclusions. You haven't been to church in years. You felt awkward around Mother Superior and now you come in here, you go to the altar; kneel, cross yourself, and meet the priest. Just what do you think he's done? I can't believe I'm saying this but you have nothing to go on."

"Only my gut... We need to interview the novices who just became nuns. I know there's something here. I feel it."

"Feel what? I think you're nuts."

"Maybe but I think there could be other novices who left the church like Suzanna because of something the Father did."

"I think you're way off base but we need to check out all the angles."

"I'm telling you Joe, I got a bad feeling about him."

"We'll investigate the priest along with her dad and ex-boyfriend... Happy?"

"Let's go."

They entered the nuns' quarters and asked to speak to some of the girls that had just graduated.

"Any of you have an inkling why Suzanna left?" asked Miller.

"No," responded Sister Margaret. "But she seemed to be struggling with something the day before taking her final vows."

"That would be Friday," said Miller.

"Yes, I saw her in the chapel praying when Father Johnson came in. They had words, at which she got up from kneeling and ran off."

"For no reason?" asked Kelby.

"Yes, and that seemed odd," said Sister Margaret.

"Thank you, Sister," responded Kelby.

Miller looked at Kelby and nodded. "You may have something here. Now we need to speak to her father, mother, and the Priest."

"What about the ex-boyfriend?"

"We'll save him for last. Maybe the parents know what's going on. Let's start with her mother. Perhaps Suzanna confided to her."

Ding dong.

"Yes?"

"Detectives Miller and Kelby; are you Mrs. Hedford?" asked Miller as they showed their identification cards and badges.

"Yes?"

"Can we come in?" asked Kelby.

"Of course, right this way."

As they entered the house, Miller said, "We need to ask you a few questions."

"Tea?" she asked.

"No, thank you. We need to clarify some things. Being Suzanna's mother, we don't know if she confided in you. We're not sure we know how to ask this but before you came to the ceremony Saturday, did you spent some time with Suzanna on Friday? We know you took pictures. Did she say anything to you? Also, did you know Father Johnson had words with her prior to the ceremony? Did you know him from before or had you just met?" asked Kelby.

"Why are you asking all these questions?"

"Because of something one of the novices told us. It seems on Friday, Father Johnson had a conversation that upset Suzanna so much that she ran from the church," said Miller.

"I don't think my conversation with Father Johnson is any of your business," Mrs. Hedford replied.

"Anything that is related to the disappearance of your daughter or this case *is* our business," said Miller.

"It's hard for me to discuss this," said Mrs. Hedford as she looked away from both detectives.

"We need a lead to go on. Just say what you have to say," replied Kelby.

"This is extremely personal... I don't know how to tell you this... Twenty-five years ago, I was a teenager attending St. Joseph's church on the other side of the Valley with my parents and little brother... I was a very impressionable young woman with a crush on a young priest."

Kelby shot Miller a look of I told you so.

"He was handsome and charismatic. I joined the choir and tried my best to get him to notice me. He finally did... We... we made love and I got pregnant. My mother sent me to a home for unwed mothers run by the nuns at another parish. I was allowed to keep my baby if I finished high school. Eventually, I married but the marriage didn't work out. My first husband wasn't ready to be a father to someone else's kid. A few years later I met a wonderful man, married him, and he adopted Suzanna as his own."

"So let me get this straight. The man who Suzanna thinks is her father isn't and the man who adopted her is her step-father. So she doesn't know who her real dad is?" replied Kelby.

"Not quite. She found out Friday that her real father was Father Johnson... Dear Lord, when I saw her, she was so distraught," said Mrs. Hedford.

"Who told her?" asked Miller.

"He did."

"That must have been why she ran from the church but why after all these years, did he tell her now?" asked Kelby.

"That's the question I've asked myself. I don't know why he would do that unless his secret was about to come out and he wanted to beat the person who knew to the punch… I don't know. I kept thinking he was being blackmailed," replied Mrs. Hedford.

"Have you talked to Father Johnson?" asked Miller.

"No, I've kept my distance since… all this time ever since I found out I was pregnant with his child."

"Who could have found out the secret?" wondered Kelby.

"If you had the baby at a home for unwed mothers run by the church, the documents are sealed but they are still there. Someone must have gotten a hold of them and decided to blackmail the priest. What reason would this person do that to convince Suzanna not to be a nun? Money?… So Father Johnson wanted to beat the blackmailer and told her first," said Miller.

"But why would Suzanna run off?" asked Kelby.

"She couldn't handle the truth… It makes sense if you know that Suzanne grew up at St. Joseph's until we moved away. She was troubled and fell into the wrong crowd. Then she decided what she wanted to do with her life and became a postulate and novice at St. Charles Church. Father Johnson moved over to St. Charles after she did to look out for her as if she were his own because she *was* his own," said her mother.

"The $64,000 question now is where did she go?" asked Miller.

"What if she went into hiding? She didn't run off because she didn't have anywhere to run," said Kelby.

"We still need to talk to the ex-boyfriend and the first husband," said Miller.

"Let's start with the ex-boyfriend."

Ring, Ring... Knock, Knock. No answer.

"Bill, I hear someone moving around inside." Miller knocked on the door again. "This is Detectives Miller and Kelby... Answer the door. We just want to talk to you."

"Leave me alone," replied a male voice.

"No one is going to hurt you... Open up," stated Kelby.

Gun shots rang out and three bullets hit the door.

Miller and Kelby hugged the door frame anticipating the gunfire. Kelby spoke into his walkie-talkie, "This is Detective Bill Kelby, we need back-up now at 1587 Chestnut Drive."

Miller and Kelby drew their guns from their shoulder holsters as they got ready to kick the door down. Kelby covered Miller as he kicked it in.

"I swear I'll kill her," said her boyfriend as he held Suzanna around the waist with a gun to her head.

"We just want to talk... No reason for anyone to get hurt," said Miller calmly.

The back-up arrived.

Kelby told the back-up to stand-by.

"Come on, put the gun down so we can talk," asked Miller.

"You're gonna arrest me for missing my meeting with my parole officer, aren't ya?"

"Not even close. We're investigating the disappearance of Suzanna Tompkins. Is this her?" Miller said.

"Yes." he said.

"Are you going to put the gun down and talk?… What's your name?" asked Miller.

"Frank."

"Okay, Frank. Toss the gun over here," said Kelby.

Looking at both detectives, he threw the gun on the floor toward Kelby and released Suzanna. He looked at her and said, "I'm sorry."

"You're going to have to go to the station for having a gun while on parole and shooting it at police officers among other charges," said Miller.

"Suzanna, why are you here?" asked Kelby.

"Frank came and got me after I called him. Father Johnson told me that he was my birth father and I was beside myself. I couldn't think. I only knew I had to get away from the church."

"Did Father Johnson tell you why he suddenly decided now to tell you?" asked Kelby.

"Yes, and I went nuts. My mother wasn't the only

woman he had sex with. There were two other women that had babies by him too. My mother's first husband found out and began to blackmail him. He wanted Father Johnson to tell me the truth before I took my final vows."

"Do you know who these other women were?" asked Kelby.

"One of them was my mother," said Frank. "My younger brother is Father Johnson's child too."

"I have a sister out there somewhere but I don't know who or where she is. It was all too much to process. I had to get away. I'm sorry I worried everyone but everything I worked so hard for had gone up in smoke," said Suzanna.

"It doesn't mean you can't be a nun. You just need to put some distance between you and Father Johnson. You could go to another parish if you decide you want to dedicate your life to the Lord," said Kelby.

"I do. That hasn't changed. But I need to forgive my mother and my… birth father. I don't know if I can."

"You need to look deep into your heart, take some time, and see if you can because if you can't, you won't be able to take your final vows," replied Kelby.

"Thank you… Detective Kelby?" said Suzanna.

"Yes?"

"How did you become so wise?" she asked.

"Life… life and being a detective for the past five years."

"God bless both of you," Suzanna said.

"Are you going to go back to your mother's house to think?" asked Kelby.

"No, I can't. I'm going to talk to the Mother Superior and ask her if I can go to one of the retreat houses to pray to decide what to do and where to go."

"What are you going to tell Mother Superior?" inquired Miller.

"The truth. I should have told her that in the beginning and saved everyone the hassle. Whatever happens to Father Johnson is his problem. He brought it on himself. I have to deal with the ramifications of my mother and his affair with her and with the two other women he had affairs with and so does he."

"Do the other children know he's their father?" asked Kelby.

"No. He needs to do the right thing and tell them. Then he needs to take whatever punishment the church gives out," said Suzanna.

"But whatever that punishment is, you need to find it in your heart to forgive him," said Kelby.

"I will but I need time."

"We'll close the case and tell Mother Superior you're okay. You realize your mother's first husband *will* be charged with blackmail," replied Miller.

"He brought that on himself too. He could have left sleeping dogs lie but instead he messed up the lives of three families and a beloved priest."

"Good luck, Suzanna," said Detectives Miller and Kelby.

"Good-bye, and thank you."

Miller turned to Suzanna's boyfriend, cuffed him and began reading Frank his rights. "Alright, you have the right to remain silent… if you give up your right, anything you say can and will be used against you in a court of law…"

_____

Previously published by CaféLit

The Prostitute Murders

"Morning Joe. How was your weekend?"

"Great. It was good having two whole days off. Cheryl and I went to the ocean. We ate brunch at a place on the beach and then went bicycling."

"Did the kids go with you?"

"No, Cheryl's mother watched them… Coffee?" asked Miller.

"Yeah, two sugars please."

Miller poured two cups of coffee taking one for himself.

"So, how was your weekend?"

"Quiet, except for Saturday night. I took Joanna to see the new James Bond movie, *Moonraker*. I figured we couldn't go wrong with Bond." said Kelby.

"So… how was the movie?"

"Good."

"Joe, Bill, can you step into my office for a minute?" said Captain Reno.

"I didn't know he was in yet," said a surprised Miller.

"He was here when I walked in a half-hour ago," replied Kelby.

"I wonder what he wants," said Miller.

"We are about to find out," said Kelby.

"Detectives Joe Miller and Bill Kelby, I'd like to introduce you to Undercover Officers Marlene Jones and Lily Hatton," said Captain Reno.

"Detectives…"

"Officers…"

"Officers Jones and Hatton have been working Vice and Narcotics for three years, the last two in Vice working to catch Johns with prostitutes. I'd like the four of you to team up for this assignment," said Reno looking at both Miller and Kelby waiting for the whining to start.

"Please don't tell us we're going to play the part of Johns to lure streetwalkers to us," said Kelby sarcastically.

"No, but you're warm. There has been a rash of prostitute killings in the area where Jones and Hatton work. The Johns hadn't gotten off scot-free by this psychopath. The ladies don't use pimps but a few are considering finding men who *will* protect them. If this happens, organized crime will move into this lucrative area," said Reno.

"If some lunatic is scaring off the Johns, it'll cut down the traffic in the area, but wait… isn't cutting down the traffic what we want? To stop the ladies from plying their trade?" said Miller not understanding the full scope of what was said.

"No, the Johns will just go elsewhere for sex. It took two years to establish an undercover presence here and to be able to bust not only prostitutes in the act but their Johns. Other than trying to stem the tide of these rendezvous, we are trying to stop the spread of STDs and unwanted pregnancies. It's not like Las

Vegas or Amsterdam where the women are checked frequently," replied Reno.

Captain Reno pulled out a folder which contained photos of badly cut-up men and dead women. "This person mutilated the Johns and strangled and cut the prostitutes. He takes great pride in choking them and rearranging their faces with a knife. With the Johns, he knocks them out and then he makes sure they could no longer function."

"What do you mean 'no longer function'?" said Miller.

"He castrates them. We have dead hookers and emasculated Johns. He wields a knife like a pro and is evolving with every occurrence, more and more violently," said Reno.

"So, he strangled all the women to death, carved up their faces, and emasculated the men leaving *them* alive… Jesus, he sounds like one angry son of a bitch," said Kelby.

"You need to contact Dr. Delmonico… Go ahead. Get a profile on him so the four of you can make a plan. I want this sadistic lunatic off the streets as soon as possible," stated Captain Reno.

"Yes, Captain," said all four of them.

"Dr. Delmonico, I'd like you to meet Undercover Officers Marlene Jones and Lily Hatton. Dr. Delmonico is the Department Psychologist," said Miller.

"It's a pleasure to meet you," said Dr. Delmonico.

"Likewise," Jones and Hatton said in unison.

"So, Joe, Bill, Ms. Jones, Ms. Hatton, what can I do for you today?" asked Dr. Delmonico.

"We have a problem. Officers Jones and Hatton have been working undercover in a sting operation posing as streetwalkers to catch Johns looking to buy sex. The area they're working has one or more unknown assailants strangling the ladies, cutting their faces, and emasculating the men," said Miller.

"Um, it appears we have we have a rage issue. His father probably walked out when he was young. Maybe it was another woman, or alcohol, or drugs; take your pick. His mother had to make a living and she didn't have any way to do it except to become a prostitute. As a boy, your suspect witnessed men coming and going in the house to have sex with his mother. He became enraged with what he saw. But at ten or eleven, he couldn't do anything about it. Now that he is an adult, he can. He probably swore he'd get even. That's why he mutilates the men," said Dr. Delmonico.

He continued, "The killing of the women is him getting back at his mother for being a prostitute. He wanted to kill her too. Maybe he *did* murder her eventually, but now he takes his rage out on the streetwalkers by strangling and cutting them up. Maybe a John cut his mother. It could be part of the revenge he wanted to get against her. It's hard to be sure but I can tell you one thing. He won't stop. At some point he may start killing the

Johns too. I can't say he'll actually do that but you need to stop this mentally ill person as soon as possible. And it is extremely dangerous for the police officers to continue to pose as prostitutes. This kind of rage can morph into all kinds of things. He's used to watching his mother and Johns that came to the house so now he's watching the Johns and prostitutes get together; he can't help but move in like a lion attacking its prey."

"The only way we can catch him is to set up a sting operation where we control everything," said Miller.

"You better *control everything* or you're going to have additional dead women and more emasculated Johns on your hands."

They told Captain Reno what Dr. Delmonico said. Captain Reno didn't like it one bit. There was no choice but to stake out the area with one of the detectives posed as a John to bring him out in the open. Captain Reno looked at both Miller and Kelby.

"Use the normal way to decide?" said Miller to Kelby.

"Yeah," replied Kelby.

Miller pulled out an Eisenhower Silver Dollar. "Heads you go, tails I go."

"Get Captain Reno to flip it… not that I don't trust you, partner, but I'm real antsy about this assignment," replied Kelby.

"Hey, I'm not crazy about it either," said Miller.

Captain Reno took the coin, looked it over, and flipped it so it fell on the office floor. The coin came up tails. Miller was the bait. He flipped it again to decide if it was either Jones or Hatton. The coin came up tails again. Jones was the pigeon.

"So, how do we set this up?" asked Miller.

"Tonight, you go to the street corner. Jones will be waiting. The area will be staked out. Miller will approach you," said Reno to Jones.

"Should I drive up in a car?" asked Miller. "I mean do you make the deals in a car with the Johns before you bust them or do you have them pull over and go up to the room and then make the deal?"

"Either way. But lately, we have been taking them to a room we've rented by the hour at the flophouse, make the deal, and arrest them right then and there. I think it will be better if Miller walks up to me and starts a conversation," said Jones.

"What about the dead girls? Where did they make the deals?" asked Reno.

"Every deal was made in the room," said Jones.

"It looks like we need to stake out the flophouse, make the business deal between the Miller and Jones, and wait for the suspect to come and try to kill them there," said Reno.

"Terrific," replied Miller.

"When do the Johns come out and look for sex?" asked Captain Reno.

"Between 10 p.m. and 4 a.m.," replied Jones.

"We'll be in place at 7 p.m. with cameras. We will have the place covered like a blanket with SWAT on the roof. Miller, you and Jones, need to make this look good from beginning to end."

"As long as you get there before I lose my masculinity," said Miller as he got up from his chair and started to pace.

"What about me? He strangles, kills, *and* cuts up the women," said Jones.

"Joe, do you have your ankle gun?" asked Kelby.

"Yes."

"Good, you might need it... Look, I'm sayin' just in case... Leave your pager here and call the missus and tell her you won't be home tonight... that you're working an undercover assignment," said Reno.

"Do I get a wireless mic?" asked Miller.

"Oh, you'll both be wired. But you need to make this look really good... Joe, you want sex and you have the dough to pay for it and Marlene wants to make some money off of you," stated Captain Reno.

"Now, it's your turn to have your chest hair itch," said Kelby.

"It's a small price to pay so I'm not turned into a eunuch... I don't think my wife would be too thrilled."

"Maybe we should ask her." Kelby snickered.

"You want a knuckle sandwich? That can be arranged," replied Miller.

Another night out to kill whores and Johns… I love it. They are the scum of the planet: the dregs of society. Every one of them deserves what they get. The women remind me of my dear departed mother who was a whore to the end and the Johns remind me of the men who traipsed in and out of our house morning, noon, and night to have sex with her. They flaunted their bodies and their sexual urges.

The body is a temple to be worshipped. It's not there to have sex with everyone that comes along. So tonight, I'll go out and kill more whores and mutilate the Johns and rid the world of more slime.

The flophouse was taken over by the detectives of the Major Case and Vice Squads. Hatton walked the street along with the other girls but they were kept back far enough to allow Jones to lure Miller to her room in plain sight. The roofs that surrounded the flophouse had men with rifles on them. The rooms on either side of Miller and Jones' room were bugged with cameras and microphones as the detectives watched from all four directions and an additional camera was focused squarely on the door. Miller's chest near the shirt pocket had a microphone that could pick up a pin drop. Jones' microphone was clipped on the inside of her push-up bra. Other than the cameras in the corners of the room, everything looked normal.

No one was to make a move unless Captain Reno gave the word. It was 10:15 p.m. Miller strolled up to Jones and said, "Hi."

"Hi."

Not knowing what to say, Miller kind of fumbled around and muttered, "I'd like to have some company tonight."

"That can be arranged," Jones responded.

"Is there a place we can go to be alone?"

"Yes, I have a room upstairs."

She took his hand and led him up the steps to the second floor of the flophouse.

A shadowy figure lurked from the alley. He watched and waited.

They wandered down the hallway with Jones opening the door to the scantily furnished dirty room. The quiet was deafening.

Jones closed the door and blurted out, "Okay, let's get the business part out of the way. What you want for your money?"

Miller wasn't expecting his fellow officer to be so blunt but he quickly composed himself and replied, "I'd like straight sex, and maybe something else… I don't know."

"That'll be $100."

"$100?"

"If you don't like the price, we don't have to do it," Jones said sarcastically.

"No… no, $100 is totally reasonable. How much time does that buy me?" asked Miller meekly.

Looking Miller straight in the eye, she said, "Half-hour. You want more time, there will be an additional charge. And you pay *before* we get started."

Miller reached into his wallet and laid two $50s on the table.

Kelby turned to Reno and said, "Jesus, she doesn't mince words."

"She's been doing this for two years. Of course, the Johns are always busted when they make the deal. This is going to be quite different."

"Captain, there's movement in the alley," one of the men on the roof said.

"Don't move in. I repeat, don't move in. It could be a vagrant or a drunk sleeping it off. Monitor and report."

"Joe, there's movement in the alley so keep alert," said Reno.

"You gotta be kidding. You better be watching our asses," Miller replied.

"Come on, loosen up, you're supposed to be enjoying yourself," said Jones as she whispered in Miller's ear while unbuttoning his shirt and massaging his chest. She pushed him on the bed, got on top of him, and muttered, "You better zip down my dress and make this look good."

Miller reached back to find the zipper and pulled it all the way down.

Her dress fell off. She was wearing a black lacy bra, a pair of black panties, with a garter and fishnet stockings. The boys watched from the other room and nearly fell out of their chairs. "Holy shit," Kelby remarked as he attempted to contain himself.

Jones pulled the dress off and got on top of Miller again.

Miller's eyes rolled into the back of his head because Jones had her breasts in his face.

She moved down toward his chest and remarked, "Wow, you have a nice hairy chest. A woman could get lost in all this wonderful hair," she said as she started rubbing it and kissing him all over.

Not knowing what to say, Miller replied, "Thank you."

"Come on," she whispered, "You gotta relax or he's gonna figure something's up and it won't be you."

Miller whispered into his shirt mic. "Come on guys, shit, I'm a happily married man. Don't you have him yet?"

"No, we don't. Keep up the charade," replied Kelby half-wanting to laugh and half-feeling sorry for his partner.

"SWAT just said someone's moving toward the front of the building. But he's just standing around, like he's checking things out," said Kelby.

"Well don't scare him off! Whatever you do! Encourage him to come into the building," said Captain Reno.

"You two, keep doing what you're doing… Joe… Joe, did you hear me?" said Kelby.

"Yeah, I heard and soon… sooner than you think, this isn't going to be an act if you catch my drift."

Jones started kissing Miller while she moved her hands down to his belt and opened it along with the pants' zipper."

Miller yelled, "Christ Almighty."

Right then, they heard a noise outside the door.

The guy stood there for a moment.

"Hold your positions," said Reno. "No one move."

The guy busted down the door. He had a cord and knife in his hands and reached around trying to put the rope around Jones' neck while wildly swinging the knife hoping to emasculate Miller.

"Go, Go, Go…" The police poured in from both rooms and grabbed the man before he could do any damage. Kelby disarmed the guy while Captain Reno slapped the cuffs on him.

I gotta get them. Don't you understand they aren't worth anything? They're scum. They have sex for money. They're the lowest of the low.

Miller stood up and zipped his pants up and started buttoning his shirt while Jones' put on her dress. Miller remarked, "I was awful close to actually getting my $100 worth."

"How do you think I felt?" said Jones. "I had never taken it this far in the past but I did what I had to do."

"Hey Jones, answer me this," asked Miller.

"Yes?"

"I know this was an undercover assignment but how far *were* you willing to go?"

"As far as I had to," she replied.

"Do me a favor: if you ever run into my wife don't say anything about this. She wouldn't understand what we were doing was necessary to catch a killer."

"But my husband does. Let me introduce you to Lieutenant Jimmy Jones, all 6'3" of him."

"Hello… nice to meet you." Miller turned to Jones. "Your husband was watching?"

"He knows this is just a job to me. I go home every night to him. And he knows this is the furthest I ever had to take an assignment. I didn't feel as comfortable as you thought I was but I was willing to do whatever I had to, to catch this psycho. I have to believe you would have done the same."

"Yeah, I guess so but no offense, I'm glad it didn't come to that." Miller started pulling on his jacket. "I can't believe this is what a cop has to do to make a living these days."

The Boxcar Murders

"Riding the rails! This is the life," said Jimmy to his partner, Willy, as they got comfortable sitting up against the back corner of the boxcar next to the caboose. It's the late 1970s. Jumping trains has gone down since the peak during the Great Depression. During the Depression, people rode the rails in search of work. Now, people jumped railcars, a dangerous practice as it was in the days of old, but nevertheless, a tradition that has continued because it's the only way to get from city to city when men are broke.

"Where there are trains, there will always be rail hoppers," said Willy. "We're not hurting anyone. We just need a lift, to get to the next town and unfortunately, we're penniless."

The train pulled into the station. Jimmy and Willy hid in the hay as they heard the whistle blow and the boxcar door wiggle.

The locomotive picked up steam and was heading out of the depot when they heard a knock as the door flew open. A stranger dressed in black looked around and spoke in a low voice. "Can I join you?"

Jimmy looked at Willy. "I guess so," said Jimmy. "Have a seat."

The man came in with a small black bag in one hand. In his other hand, he had a sawed-off shotgun.

The two men stared in disbelief. "Look Mister, we didn't do nothing wrong except take a ride in this car. We'll get off. Please, we don't want no trouble," said Willy.

The man in black didn't say a word before he shot both men dead. Then, he opened the railcar and jumped out leaving the bodies behind.

When the train pulled into the last station and a check was made of all the cars, Jimmy and Willy's bodies were discovered. The train had gone two hundred miles. There wasn't a clue where they were killed. This was the sixth and seventh rail murders in the past two weeks. Hobos or rail hoppers, as they were called, were being murdered not just in Los Angeles but wherever there were freight trains in California. It might be seven locally but when other agencies pulled their data in the last two months, it was forty-three. This person was out to rid the population of hobos and no one knew why.

Joe Miller and Bill Kelby of the Major Case Squad were contacted. They visited the crime scene.

"Jesus Christ, a sawed-off shot gun at close range. Not much left of him," said Miller.

"Whatever the reason is we have a guy who is playing vigilante of the railroads. We need to talk to Dr. Delmonico," replied Kelby.

"Joe, Bill, what can I do for you today?"

"We have a serial killer on our hands. It looks like

he enters the boxcar after a train has left the station. He shoots the victim or victims with a sawed-off shotgun. It appears he is out to rid the railroads of all the vagrants. I realize they're illegal rail riders but this is ridiculous. What do you make of it?" said Miller.

"It's hard to say by the little you've told me but let me give you my take of what kind of person I think you're dealing with. I believe the person most likely had a father who left his family while he was young, maybe eight or nine. The father was over his head in responsibilities: a wife, a kid or two, probably a mortgage so he took off for a simpler life of riding the rails which meant he abandoned the family. The boy had to grow up fast, be the man, maybe leave school to go to work to bring money home to help support the family. But he vowed revenge. He decided when he grew up and was able to leave home, he was going to ride the rails and kill his father, but so far he hasn't found him. Because his anger is white hot, he goes into a blind range and takes his hostility out on every transient he sees. Each one reminds him of his father so he kills over and over never getting the release he needs," stated Dr. Delmonico.

"You mean he's going to continue to kill until we find him and stop him? Do you realize how many rail lines and track we're talking about?" said Miller.

"Have all the killings occurred in one state?" asked Dr. Delmonico.

"Yes," said Kelby.

"Well, that's a start. Have they occurred on one rail line?"

"No, just the two big ones. Union Pacific and Burlington Northern Santa Fe," said Miller.

"I don't envy you. You have hundreds of miles to cover. If I were you, I'd go back to the first killing. Mark the location. See which train it's associated with and then check where it stops, like railroad crossings and water stops because usually vagrants get on moving cars near stops. However, if this is a young man, and he hasn't adapted to the life style yet, he might be getting on at towns hiding near the trains until they're ready to pull out. I'd start there."

"Thanks, Dr. Delmonico," said Miller and Kelby.

"Jesus, Miller, do you have any idea the amount of work we're looking at?" said Kelby.

"Let's go back to the office and lay it all out on the whiteboard and a map," said Miller.

Damn, two more are dead and I'm no closer to killing that bastard father of mine. He can't be dead. I won't let myself believe he's dead. He needs to pay for what he did to me and my family.

This picture I have of him is old and faded. He's been gone fifteen years but I'd recognize that son of a bitch anywhere. Mom worked herself to death and I had to drop out of school and take care of my baby sister. And what happens? She got hooked on meth and knocked up at the same time. I had no life… NO LIFE because of that gluttonous pig who abandoned us. Well, he's gonna get his… I'm gonna make sure he pays.

"Kelby, this is like working a puzzle with most of the pieces gone… Shit. We need one lead, just one, where someone suspicious is seen getting on a train," exclaimed a frustrated Miller.

"You know how many people hop trains every day?" replied Kelby.

"I mean one and then another so at least two get on together. The last murders were two guys together and a third joined so the third was the murderer."

"The problem is we've dusted for prints and mostly came up with the dead guys. There were a partial set of prints that were unknown so we have to hope he gets picked up for something else and then we could match his prints. We need to get him on a totally unrelated charge," replied Kelby.

"I wouldn't get my hopes up," said Miller as he put his head in his hands.

I'm almost out of money. It's time to rob a liquor store or a market and get some cash and food.

I'll jump off the train as it pulls into the station. No one saw me as I was in the next to the last car. I prefer those cars because that's where most of the vagrants hang out. Bums like my father was… is. I have hung onto the dream that I will find him someday and finish him off… blow him away, just like I did to all the rest of those scum bastards that ride the rails.

"Alright, everybody just stay nice and still. No one move and no one will get hurt! I just want the money in the register. Put it in the bag along with sandwiches, chips, and some sodas. No one has to be a hero… You over there, no movement. Don't touch anything!"

Too late. The store clerk triggered the silent alarm and for that, he had to die. BANG… went one barrel of the shotgun. "I've gotta get out of here. Give me the bag," Danny screamed.

He took the bag and ran out the front door. Sirens blared in the background. He ran toward the boxcar. The train pulled out of the station when he got on but he wasn't alone. He opened the door and there were two bums sitting there.

"Hi. I'm Leroy. This is my friend, Bobby."

"Leave me alone," replied Danny.

"You're not very sociable," said Leroy.

"I just want to be left alone to eat; then I'll leave."

There were two. Danny only had one barrel of his shotgun loaded. He had to wait until they went to sleep and then he would kill them both.

"Do you have any extra sandwiches?" asked Bobby.

"NO! I haven't eaten in two days. These are mine," said Danny.

"Sorry, we thought you'd share," said Leroy.

"Nobody ever shared with me. Get your own."

The train accelerated. The two bums eyed Danny's every move in the hopes of stealing his food.

"Look, either one of you tries to take my food, I'll kill you, you see. I have a sawed-off shotgun under my coat and I *will* use it."

Leroy started to make his way over to see and Danny pulled the gun out from under his coat.

"Look Mister, we don't want any trouble," said Leroy.

"Then stay on your side, got it!" exclaimed Danny.

He finished eating; then loaded the other barrel. "Now, there's one for each of you. Don't cross me or you'll both get it."

"I knew we should have jumped him when he first came in, said Bobby."

"Well, you aren't going to get a chance," and with that Danny blew a hole in each of them, first Leroy and then Bobby. The sound of the train's engine covered the noise of the blast.

Miller and Kelby arrived at the grocery store. Forensics matched the partial fingerprints from the train. "Our killer got off the train to eat, so where is the nearest train?" asked Kelby.

Getting impatient, Miller shouted, "Does someone know where the nearest train tracks are, which train it is, and where it's going?"

Miller received his information and ordered a helicopter, and roadblocks. "Handle with extreme caution. He is probably riding toward the rear of the train, in a boxcar. Stop the train and surround it but don't move in."

The train started to slow down. Danny planned to get off but when he opened the door, he saw cops everywhere. "You aren't taking me alive. You hear that," he said.

"There's nowhere for you to run," replied Miller.

"Then I'll take as many of you with me as I can."

The boxcar door opened next to Danny's car. A bum yelled out. "Hey, what's going on here? Can't a man get some sleep?"

"Get back in and close the door," screamed Kelby.

"Not till you tell me, what's all the fuss about? You're holding up the train. We've got a schedule to keep."

That voice… there's something familiar in that voice. Oh, it can't be. My deadbeat Dad is in the car next to me. Shit… so close and yet so far.

"Close the door, and go lie down," shouted Miller.

"Yeah," screamed Danny. "Go back inside."

"You coming out," shouted Kelby.

"Yeah, in a minute," said Danny as he took his shotgun out and prepared to use it by reloading it.

"Throw down your weapons," yelled Miller.

Danny blew a hole in the side of wooden boxcar closest to the next car. He squeezed through the hole and then blew another hole in the car that contained his father. The cops started firing back. Danny took a handgun out of the black bag and returned fire. He was shot in the shoulder but made it into the car and confronted his father.

"He's in the boxcar next door," said Kelby.

Danny threw away the pistol and quickly reloaded the shotgun.

"You old bastard, you ruined my life," screamed Danny.

"Who are you?" the old bum replied.

"You don't even recognize your own son?" said Danny.

"Son? I don't have a son or a wife for that matter," stated the old bum.

"Yeah, fifteen years ago you abandoned your family," exclaimed Danny.

"I don't know who you think I am."

"You're my father. You don't even recognize your son?" said Danny.

Meanwhile Miller and Kelby with SWAT moved into position with guns drawn. "This is your last warning; throw down your gun. You're surrounded."

Danny put the shotgun barrel under his father's neck and was about the pull the trigger when the door opened.

"Drop it, now," said Miller.

"You win again you old bastard. I can't believe it," said Danny.

Miller put his gun against Danny's head. "Drop it or so help me I *will* kill you."

Danny dropped his gun. Kelby cuffed him and took him into custody.

"You're a lucky man," stated Miller to the old bum.

"I guess I am. What a pity he turned out so bad."

"Is he or isn't he your son?" asked Miller.

"I left home fifteen years ago. I had a son named Danny so it could be him. I… I just don't know."

They left the hobo in the boxcar. He opened another bottle of whiskey and started drinking it. After they put Danny in the police car, Miller turned to Kelby and said, "The old man doesn't even know if that was his kid. How sad is that?"

Kelby responded, "Why do you think he thought this old man was his father?"

"Dr. Delmonico would know for sure but I think he wanted it so bad so he believed that old beggar was his dad because his killing spree would finally come to an end. He needed to kill his father to come full circle," said Miller.

"I feel sorry for all those men who died. What a waste! And the old man didn't even know if he was his son. Sad," replied Kelby.

Previously published by CaféLit

The Food Critic's Murder

It is my distinct pleasure to be your new food critic. The prior critic, Mr. Johansen, has retired as his eyesight and poor taste had caught up to him. He visited local restaurants for years and always thought the food was excellent. How exceptionally boring! I will have an opportunity to revisit these places and I will give you my opinion which I believe will greatly differ from his. Not only are these places overrated but overpriced for the portions received. In most of the places, I will also review the beer, wine, and mixed drinks, if available. I prefer French wine but will sample what is at hand. Stay tuned for my first review.

Jean Claude Dubois was happy with his typed introductory column and was extremely pleased with himself, being the narcissist that he was.

I'll shake things up in Los Angeles. My column will be in the Sunday Food section of their biggest paper, The Journal. After my reviews come out, the slobs who own these places will get on their hands and knees to beg for another opportunity to please me. I'll have so much power over these peons. How glorious that will be!

Early Monday morning Miller and Kelby came into work and this Monday Miller brought the Sunday food column with him.

"Hey Kelby, do you read the food section of the paper?"

120

"No, the wife does. I'm the sports section kind of guy," replied Kelby half-laughing.

"Me too, but something weird happened in this Sunday's paper and I brought it in to show you."

"Well, I'm waiting. What was weird?" said Kelby.

"The old food critic is gone and some new hotshot has taken his place and he could be potential trouble. You gotta read his opening column," said Miller.

Kelby read the column and agreed with his partner. "This guy could tick off a lot of people…"

"But, it's just words… Aw come on, you don't think when he actually starts reviewing these places, he'll stir up trouble and someone might off him?" said Miller.

"It's possible. People I know used to read the old guy and if the new guy gives a restaurant a bad review, it could cause people to stop going there. The old guy never gave horrible reviews. My wife said that he would try several dishes and maybe he wouldn't like one but he wouldn't focus on that. This guy sounds like he's out for blood," replied Kelby.

"There's nothing we can do until, if, or when, something happens. Come on, we have real cases to deal with," responded Miller.

The next six weeks, Mr. Dubois visited Los Angeles' favorite restaurants and wrote his scathing reviews.

To La Bamba de La Rosa Mexican Food Restaurant:
The atmosphere reminded me of a stable where donkeys were housed. In fact, it smelled the same way. The salsa was watery and tasteless. It went well with the overly-salted tortilla chips. I ordered a chicken burrito and a beef taco. Some poor bird gave its life for that burrito. The meat was scarce and what meat I could find was poor quality. The beef taco was made from ground beef. It made the shell soggy and impossible to pick up and eat. The margarita had too much salt on the rim and not enough alcohol to kill the taste of the bad food. All in all, it was an unsatisfactory experience.

"I think the war of the food critic has begun," said Miller.

"Why?" responded Kelby.

"You didn't see the paper yesterday?" asked Miller.

"No."

"He started off with that little Mexican place the missus and I go to on occasion. He ripped up the burritos and tacos and said the margaritas were light on the alcohol," replied Miller.

"Was he right?" inquired Kelby.

"I didn't think so but we haven't been there recently," said Miller.

"Maybe the quality has gone down… you think?" asked Kelby.

"I don't know. But I do think he's here to stir up trouble and he started with a favorite neighborhood restaurant. This situation will become nasty awful fast if he continues on this vein," said a concerned Miller.

To Marcharelli's Italian Restaurante:
The owners tried to recreate a piece of Italy as their menu says. What part of Italy? I say, it must be the boot, the bottom of the boot in particular. The spaghetti wasn't cooked enough for my taste. The menu said "al dente", which meant firm but not hard. Someone forgot to tell the chef the meaning. I asked for meat sauce. I received uncooked lumps on top of my hard noodles. The eggplant had too much breading. When I cut into it, I couldn't find the eggplant. Then they put a healthy portion of cheese and sauce on it to cover their mistake. I decided to have a glass of red wine with my meal. It was their "Vino de Casa", or House Wine as it is known which tasted like vinegar. So, I couldn't even kill the taste of the bad food with alcohol.

"Hey Miller did you see the food critic's review of that little Italian place on 5th Street over the weekend?" said Kelby.

"I did and he raked that place over the coals. I've been there and the food isn't anywhere as bad as he said. In fact, I like their eggplant," replied Miller.

"I told you he was here to make trouble."

"This was week two. Let's wait and see what he does next week," said a half-worried Miller.

The Old American Burger Company and Bandstand: I figured I'd at least get a decent meal here but I was wrong. I ordered a burger with no seasoning; French fries no salt, and a microbrew beer on tap. Either the order was written down wrong even though I made the server repeat the order back to me and confirm they could make it "my way" or the cook couldn't read. What I received was a charcoal blackened briquette of a piece of meat; oh how that poor cow gave its life for that burger. Then, the burger must have sat under a warming light for quite a while because it was served ice cold. I kept thinking how was it possible to get a burnt cold burger? Maybe this was a Los Angeles phenomenon. The fries had extra salt instead of no salt. The only redeeming part of the meal was the beer. She actually brought it without spilling any of it, and it had a head on it.

"Holy cows Kelby; my kids went nuts when we told them what he said about their favorite burger place," stated Miller.

"Are you and the wife still going to go there?" Kelby looked at his partner with a raised eyebrow.

"Well to be honest, I don't know. After this review, maybe not," replied Miller.

124

"You're going to let the critic think for you?" said Kelby who drunk some coffee and practically spit it out being surprised at what his partner said.

"Well, he's right about the fries. I always did think they were too salty but the wife and kids liked them so I said okay."

"If more people thought like you, the place won't have any customers," said Kelby.

"Nah, that won't happen… will it?" asked Miller.

Three Headed Dragon Bar and Grill:
I'm not a fan of Asian food because most of the menu is rice and noodle dishes so I purposely stay away from those and order something else. I picked two meat dishes plus egg rolls and egg drop soup in the hopes of having leftovers the next day. I should have known better than to order so much food. I couldn't even give it to my neighbor's dog. What a waste. The soup was watery with bits of water chestnuts but where was the egg? You needed a microscope to find it. The egg rolls were hot but mushy inside. I had to ask three times for hot mustard and then they gave me two measly packets. Is there an embargo with China on mustard these days? My main dishes were BBQ pork which was fatty and stringy. Again, this is another place with a poor quality meat. I tried the Honey Walnut Chicken which was a little too sweet for me but the chicken was white meat and the nuggets were good size. If it had less coating on it, it would have been good. I had hot

green tea but refills weren't free. For the prices they charge, can't they give free refills on the tea? That's appalling. I had a bottle of beer which was good since the only way they could have ruined the beer was it not being cold and I saw that their beers were kept in the cooler which is why I ordered it.

"Oh no, not another horrible review," said Miller.

"Yeah and my wife loves Three Headed Dragon. We usually get the Mongolian beef and fried rice but he is right about the egg rolls. I never did like them," said Kelby.

"Would you go back?"

"Probably and just order what we always do. But I can see your point. People are going to shy away from trying these places that are being singled out as having bad food and paying a lot of money for it," replied Kelby.

Le Petite Fleur French Restaurant:
Being French, I hold these places to a higher standard. So I tried three standard French items starting with French onion soup which I absolutely adore. This place dropped an entire salt shaker in it ruining that delicate onion flavor. The next supposed delicacy I tried was Salmon en papillote which is fish delicately wrapped in paper to hold the moisture in. Someone forgot the paper. It was dry and tasteless. The salmon needed, dare I say it, lemon and dill? They should be ashamed.

Finally Lamb shank navarin which is lamb that is cooked low and slow until it melts in the mouth but instead this critic received lamb that was cooked high and fast and resembled the burger I had at the American restaurant. The only highlight of the evening was being able to order French wine which I knew would be good so I ended up spending another evening drinking my dinner.

"Hey Miller, you ever eat at the French place?" asked Kelby.

"Are you kidding? I couldn't afford having an appetizer there."

"I think people who have money may think twice before returning."

"After a review like that, I think you might be right, partner. What a shame," replied Miller.

Eggs Are Our Specialty:
I had to assume that anything for breakfast that contained eggs and their side dishes were their specialty. Wrong! The chickens gave up their eggs under duress and the food tasted like it. I didn't think I could get rubber eggs but I did. I ordered two simple meals. Two eggs over easy, hash browns with no salt, and sourdough toast dry, butter and jelly on the side. I got two eggs over hard, hash browns that had more salt than the saltshaker on the table, and white toast burnt with extra butter. I sent it back. I ordered a cheese omelet,

with pancakes, no butter. I received the omelet but couldn't find the cheese, and pancakes with butter. I truly think that the waiter didn't hear what was said or wrote down the opposite to piss me off. I sent the meal back and just had coffee. At least the coffee was black and hot and they left the carafe on the table so I could have refills whenever I wanted. Too bad, it was morning. I could have used a drink after the lack of a good meal.

"I have to admit he was right about Eggs Are Our Specialty. I haven't eaten there in years. The eggs *are* rubber. You can't ever get them cooked the way you want, the hash browns are too salty and I always ask for sourdough toast and they brought me white. After a couple of times of that nonsense, I stopped going there," said Miller.

"See, if enough people agree with him, these places will go out of business," replied Kelby.

"Well, maybe some of them should, if they serve bad or cold food or the drinks are watered down or have rotten service. Restaurants must be competitive. If I'm paying good money, I expect things to be right."

"I guess he found a convert in you but I suspect he is walking on thin ice. He better watch his step."

"I called this meeting of the Restaurants and Businessmen Association to bring to your attention the negative publicity we received by Mr. Jean Claude Dubois' column in the Sunday newspaper. No one, and I mean no one, will escape his vitriolic attack on our restaurants. He looks for the slightest thing wrong and blows it out of proportion. I know my business is off 30% since he published his review. I can't handle that kind of loss. It's as if he wanted all of us to go out of business," said the owner of the Italian Restaurant, Mr. Antonio Canali.

He continued, "Mr. Dubois reviews everything from the atmosphere, to the temperature of the food, to the consistency of the food, and what beverage he pairs it with which is his choice not the restaurant's. We're being dragged through the mud by this columnist. Bluntly stated, this dumb bastard took over from a man of integrity. We have a narcissistic son of a bitch with a God complex to put up with. If only he would give constructive criticism but instead he rips the food and restaurant up beyond repair. I would be happy to give him another meal if what he said was true but it isn't."

Mr. Canali stopped for a moment, composed himself and continued on, "We must find a way to neutralize the bad publicity. I have complained to his newspaper but believe it or not since he started, he's responsible for selling more papers than the last man because people can't wait to see which restaurant he's going to review next. I did some digging. He was run out of the last town he worked in. It was smaller than Los Angeles and the restaurant owners had enough of his nonsense, got together, and convinced him to leave town."

"How?" said the owner of the Egg Restaurant. "They threatened him?"

"Basically, yes."

"Are you saying we should do the same thing?" said the Egg Restaurant owner.

"I'm saying we need to do whatever it takes to preserve our livelihoods. If things don't improve, I'll have to lay off half my staff and possibly close. I don't want to give this puffed-up peacock the satisfaction..." replied Mr. Canali.

Pierre, owner of the French restaurant, raised his hand and asked to speak.

"Yes, Pierre, you have the floor," said Mr. Canali.

"I would like to adjourn this meeting to another location. One that is more private to discuss a possible solution," he replied.

"I second the motion. All say, aye that we adjourn and move the meeting," said Mr. Canali.

"Aye," replied everyone in the restaurant.

The meeting was moved to the basement of Pierre's restaurant after it closed at 1 a.m.

"Thank you for coming," Pierre began. "This basement is solid cement and since we are talking about a sensitive subject... well, the walls have ears where we were... I believe that we need to do more than just drive Mr. Dubois out because wherever he goes, he'll it do it again to other restaurateurs. He gets satisfaction in hurting hard-working business people. So, I suggest we draw straws to see who has the responsibility of killing him."

"What? You can't be serious?" said Jose Mendez owner of the Mexican restaurant.

"I am deadly serious, no pun intended. Short straw does the deed but we're all in this together and if it's done correctly, the police won't know who to charge with his murder," replied Pierre.

"No, they'll charge everyone here because we all had a hand in it," said the burger place owner.

"Ah, but you ask what about opportunity? Each one of us will establish an alibi, whether it is working, home with family, at the ballgame, somewhere else other than with him when he dies," stated Pierre without emotion.

"And what do you intend to kill him with?" said Jose Mendez.

"He lives alone. He comes into our establishments alone. He eats alone. He probably has many enemies, not just us that want him dead. His passion is wine although he drinks beer and other alcoholic drinks. There are several poisons that can be put in his beverage without leaving a trace." Pierre smiled.

"Certainly not in one of *our* restaurants," said the owner of the Chinese Restaurant.

"What if someone breaks into his house, coats

one of his wine glasses with brucine, allows it dry, and waits for him to pour himself a glass of wine when no one is around. The brucine dries clear on the inside of the glass. It goes back into solution once the wine hits it. He drinks it. He drops dead and it looks like a heart attack. Once he's dead, we pull the glass he drank from and replace it with another empty wine glass with the bottle next to the glass. The police test both the bottle and glass and come up empty. Voila. The autopsy comes back as a heart attack."

"I… don't… know…" said Jose Mendez hesitantly.

"Do any of you have a better plan?… What do you want to do?… Nothing? Let our businesses die? All because some narcissistic jackass waltzes into town and wants to make a name for himself? I'll do the deed. But we have to be unanimous on this, not tell our families, *and* not speak of this to another living soul," said Pierre. "We need to vote. Do I hear a dissenting vote?"

The business owners sat silently each agreeing one by one to go along with the plan. "Then all we need to do is to meet again to determine the time and day. I think it should be done mid-week. Someone needs to find out where he lives… what his schedule is. What nights he's home. Stuff like that. I'll get the brucine and the wine. Since he hates California wine so much, I will supply the finest French wine. Each one of us must go out and buy a bottle of French wine the week we do it. We must throw suspicion all around. Finding out what he drinks would be a big help but, if not, finding out where he buys his wine is just as good. Just not all of us go to the same place and buy a bottle of the same wine. We don't want anything to arouse suspicion on each of us by the police. We'll all be suspects but the key is that we have alibis. Even me, I will have an alibi by going to Dodger Stadium that night."

"Are you sure this will work?" said Jose Mendez.

"No, but not doing anything is *not* a solution. You have your assignments. We will meet here next Tuesday night. Adjourned," said Pierre.

André, Pierre's nephew, was the youngest and most agile of the aging restaurant owners. Thirty-five and athletic, André found out where Jean Claude lived and staked out his place, followed him to and fro, and watched his every move. He saw where he bought wine and went back to report everything to the other owners.

Each made arrangements for their alibis and the restaurant owners purchased identical bottles of wine from different stores. The day came. André followed Jean Claude to the restaurant he was about to ruin then quickly went to his apartment. He got in by using a credit card and slid it along the lock. He put gloves on before touching anything making sure to wipe the door and knob clean. He took the wine glass that sat on the table next to Jean Claude's bottle of wine and coated the inside with brucine and waited for it to dry. André went down the hall and watched for Jean Claude to return. He came back, went into his place, opened the wine, and drank an entire glass, not even savoring it.

The food tonight was so unbelievably bad that no one will ever return to this place after I write my review. He poured another glass of wine and drank half of it when he grabbed his chest like he was having a heart attack.

"Damn food," he muttered. He went to the cupboard and pulled down some bicarbonate of soda. He mixed it up and drank it but the pain got so bad that he passed out on the floor, dead from a heart attack. André heard the thunk and let himself in. He took the glass with the brucine and replaced it with a clean one. He pressed Jean Claude's fingerprints on the glass and placed it by the bottle. He looked at the dead man and said, "Bon appétit. Have a nice trip to hell."

André checked the hall before he left the room and then went out the window as planned.

When Jean Claude didn't show up to dictate his column to the typist the next day, the paper sent someone to his place to check on him and found him dead on the floor. The coroner came. CSI dusted for prints and took pictures.

The Major Case squad was called but with no

evidence it was a homicide; they had nothing to go on.

Looking at the body, Miller said, "I told you someone was going to off him."

"You don't know that until the autopsy comes back," stated Kelby.

"Whatever the person or persons used, I bet it won't show up on the tox screen."

"Death by heart attack," said the coroner. "Tox screen came up empty. Sorry, I can't help you boys. I ran every known substance including pufferfish poison like you had on that other case. Nothing. Zip. Nada."

"Any chance it was potassium chloride?" asked Kelby.

"No needle marks. I checked thoroughly," said the coroner shaking his head. If it was murder, they did an excellent job covering their tracks.

"What about digitalis?" questioned Miller.

"He wasn't on any heart medicine. According to you, he had so many enemies but I can't give you a cause of death except a heart attack. Sorry guys."

"I hate to say it but someone has just got away with murder," said Kelby.

"You're probably right but without any forensic evidence which I don't have for you, you don't have a case," replied the coroner.

"I'd bet my pension it's murder," said Miller.

"Me too, partner, but without the evidence, we can't pick anyone up and question them."

"Maybe we need to go over the room again?" asked Miller.

"CSI went over it three times. There were no fingerprints other than the dead man's, no sign of a struggle, and no indication that he died other than from natural causes," Kelby remarked.

"You know several people who had motives to get rid of him."

"Maybe, but there just isn't any evidence to go on. Let it go," said Kelby.

"Damn," said Miller.

The coroner signed the death certificate as natural causes. He didn't know to look for brucine.

Previously published by CaféLit

The Used Car Salesmen Murders

"Hey Joe?"

"Yeah," said Miller sipping a cup of coffee.

"Are you still thinking about buying a used car?" asked Kelby.

"Yeah, I need another one. The wife is doing more with the kids. There are ballet lessons for my daughter and softball practice for my son. Even if she offers to carpool with one or two of the other moms, and on those days, I leave my car and you pick me, we still can't make it work."

"Where have you looked?" asked Kelby.

"Not too many places. A couple of lots near my house," replied Miller.

"Have you tried Cal Worthington[2]?"

"No, in fact I hadn't considered going there. And I see his ads all the time at night while I'm watching TV. I still want to compare prices and financing. I really hate buying a used car. I know what I want but those pushy salesmen drive me insane," replied Miller.

"Hey Joe, Bill, can you step into my office?" said Captain Reno.

Miller and Kelby went into their Captain's office to see what he wanted.

---

[2] A real life Ford auto dealership that advertised from the 1960s through the 1990s in the Los Angeles area. He was very popular with his dog, Spot, which usually wasn't a dog but a tiger, monkey, elephant, etc. He had a popular jingle.

Reno closed the door, looked at Miller, and said, "I couldn't help hear you're considering buying a used car."

"Yeah, the wife and I are having problems sharing," responded Miller.

"Good, because I have a case for the two of you."

"What is it?" asked Kelby.

"Someone is stabbing used car salesmen to death," said Reno.

"Seriously?" said Miller.

"Yeah, the first one came in off the wire from San Francisco a week ago. Since it was out of our jurisdiction we didn't give it a thought. It was at Ralph Williams' Bayshore Chrysler Plymouth.[3]

"We didn't link it to the one down here until they put out on the wire that someone appeared to be targeting used car salesmen," replied Reno.

"Any clues?" asked Kelby.

"No fingerprints, and no copy of a driver's license, which would be necessary if someone wanted to take a car for a spin. Absolutely nothing. The procedure is to ask for a driver's license when someone wants to test drive a car but that didn't happen. So we suspect the guy came in to talk to the

---

[3] Another true dealership that sold cars and made commercials similar to Cal Worthington. This guy had a German Sheppard named Storm who slept on the hood of the cars while the TV cameras rolled.

salesman, and before a test drive could happen, he stabbed him. I want you to go to the car lot and check out the facts," said Reno.

"Is there any other information you can give us? I mean what does some person do… walk around the lot, find a salesman, and stab him? Does he make off with a car? If so, did he keep it?" asked Miller.

"Both murders were the same. He killed each salesman with a knife in the common area of the dealership and then took the keys and drove off in a random car. He traveled about three miles and then abandoned it. The cars were dusted for prints and they were clean. We put this out on the wire to see if any other cities in California that had any murders, plus neighboring cities including, Las Vegas, Reno, Phoenix, San Diego, and Portland and it came back zero. The motivation isn't stealing the cars because he dumps them a few blocks from the dealership. He's out to kill the salesmen; however, he showed his power by stealing the cars *after* he killed the salesmen. *And* he doesn't leave any fingerprints," said Captain Reno.

Miller and Kelby walked out of Captain Reno's office perplexed.

"This doesn't make any sense at all. We need to talk to Dr. Delmonico," said Miller.

"Hi Joe, Bill, are you on a new case and if so, what can I help you with today?"

"Well, we have a bit of a perplexing case," stated Kelby.

"I'm ready," replied Dr. Delmonico.

"We have a person who has killed two used car salesmen. We put it out on the wire and those were the only two places." said Miller.

"I think what we have here is a person, more likely a man, that had a tremendous loss in his life. Perhaps a wife or a girlfriend or even a child was killed or maimed in a car accident. It was the kind of accident that could have been avoided because in his mind he was sold a lemon. The car might have had brake failure or a tire blowout, or an engine fire. Maybe he bought a car that was on a recall list and he didn't know it or worse yet the car wasn't fixed in a recall because the original owners were sent letters that said there might be problems and they didn't take it in. Maybe the original owner wasn't notified. Two cars come to mind: the Ford Pinto and the Chevy Malibu… It doesn't matter why; it matters that he'll keep killing used car salesmen until you stop him," replied Dr. Delmonico.

"But unfortunately, we do not have the manpower to stake out every used car lot in the state of California," stated Kelby."

"You may not have to. I think on this case you need to set a trap for him. Lure him to a specific used car lot with one of you as the bait."

"Oh, no, I've had enough of being the bait for psychos to last a lifetime," said Miller shaking his head.

"The *only* way to stop this man is to bring him to you. I read in the paper that the killings took place at flamboyant car lots advertising used cars. You need to create a third lot where you control all the circumstances. You said you haven't heard about any other killings."

"No, the information on the wire showed these two killings so far," said Kelby.

"That's the key: so far. He's just begun but he will continue. You must stop him before he really blows this out of proportion. I suggest you set the scene by steering this killer into one place."

"And just how do we bring this maniac into killing at a certain lot," asked Miller.

"You contact some dealerships in the area to see if they would be willing to go along with a plan of luring the killer to you. They need to set up a media campaign. Get the same networks involved that do the Cal Worthington commercials. A week's worth of ads should be enough. If the dealership won't pay for it, get the mayor to open the purse strings, but this is the only way. If you don't, there're going to be a lot of dead salesmen in the not too distant future… *And* one of you should be the announcer," replied Dr. Delmonico.

"Not me," said Miller looking at Kelby. "It's your turn after I spent the evening with Officer Jones."

"Well whosever's turn it is, you better decide and do it fast."

141

"You're sure it's a he?" asked Kelby.

"Pretty sure. I thought you might ask me for help so I asked to see the autopsy report. It took a strong person to stab both salesmen. One man was attacked from the front and one was from behind. He stabbed both in the midsection, not in a fleshy area. The one in the front was stabbed in and upwards to the heart with such a force that the victim was dead before he hit the floor and the second was stabbed in the back in a powerful downward motion that nearly eviscerated him."

"That's terrific and you want one of us to be the pigeon?" replied Kelby.

"It's the only way," replied Dr. Delmonico.

"Can you give an estimate of the suspect's height?" asked Miller.

"Maybe 6' to 6'2". Beyond that, no. Perhaps the coroner can help."

"We asked, but he had nothing to add except what you said," said Kelby.

"Work the profile that I've given you and you should be able to apprehend this distressed individual before he strikes again, but don't wait too long," said Dr. Delmonico.

"How can you say distressed? He's a nut; he murdered two men," replied Kelby.

"I say he's distressed because I believe before he started on his killing spree, he had this tremendous loss in his life. He was normal like you and me. He went to work, had a home life with a girlfriend or wife, maybe a child and then it was all taken away. The man snapped pure and simple. He must be stopped and hopefully not killed. *If you can't stop him, do what you must…*" said Dr. Delmonico.

"Thank you, Dr. Delmonico," replied both Miller and Kelby.

"Well, Captain, that's what the shrink told us," said Kelby.

"Then I'll get with OK Used Cars and their camera crew to see when we can film a couple of commercials and get the stations to air them for the next week. Kelby, you or Miller need to figure it out who will be the spokesman."

Miller shook his head, looked at his partner and said, "I was the bait the last time. It's only fair that you be it this time."

Kelby cringed as he reluctantly agreed he would do it with Miller being his back-up.

The boys met the camera crew, went over the script, and shot two commercials. They were on the order of the Cal Worthington commercials except Kelby did not have any animals in it, not even a cat. It was hard enough to get him to relax and read the copy printed on cue cards located beneath the cameras.

Since the murders happened at night, Kelby went to the dealership at 5 p.m. expecting the murderer would show up after dark. Miller wasn't far behind sitting on the floor in one of the sales offices when Kelby was inside the showroom and lying down on the front seat of one of the cars when he was outside in the parking lot.

Kelby wore a wire and a thin polyethylene knife resistant vest under his shirt and suit jacket as he strolled back and forth through the dealership. Only the maintenance man was on the lot, acting like he was hosing down the outside pavement but he was actually a plain clothes detective named Roberts who was there to back-up Miller. Across the street, on the roof, were six SWAT officers. They were called in to be extra eyes scoping out the area. The sharpshooters were poised to take out any potential threat on a moment's notice. Everyone could hear a pin drop. The microphone was attached to Kelby's chest. Kelby was surprised they didn't hear his heart beating a mile a minute. He'd been on a lot of assignments but this one scared the absolute shit out of him to the point of him sweating buckets.

Waiting… that was the worst possible scenario… will he show up? Will he take the bait?

Kelby walked into the showroom from the parking lot. A couple had been by to look at cars and left, so except for his partner and the maintenance man both watching his every move, he was alone. He had his .38 tucked into the back part of his waistband and his .22

in his ankle holster. Maybe the perpetrator wouldn't come tonight. Then he'd have to go through this tomorrow night and the night after that. Kelby didn't know if he could take the stress. Miller made his way from the outside car lot to the inside sales department office, watching his partner's every move.

Kelby heard a door open and close by the service department. The service department closed at five and everyone had left. *Oh dear God, this might be him.*

"I hear something near the service department," whispered Kelby into his microphone.

"We don't have eyes. We're moving into position," replied the SWAT Captain.

"Joe," said Kelby. "Joe, are you there?… Oh, for Christ's sake… are you there… JOE???"

"I'm here, Bill."

Cross traffic chatter was picked up on the microphone.

"Do you have eyes on Bill?" asked the SWAT Captain to Miller.

"Yes, I do," responded Miller. "Roberts, Roberts… shut off the water and move closer to the showroom. Keep your gun out."

"On my way."

"Roberts, can you see Bill?" asked Miller.

"Got him," said Roberts.

"What's he doing?" questioned Miller.

"Walking around the showroom."

"*Where* exactly?" asked Miller.

"On the driver's side near the white Camaro *in* the showroom," replied Roberts.

"Bill, Roberts and Miller are watching you," said the SWAT Captain. "Do you still hear footsteps?"

"Yes… Dear God… now they're coming from the parts department and they're heading my way."

"Miller, Roberts, do you copy?"

"Yes," they said in unison.

Kelby was shaking as he walked around the showroom. "Is someone there?… Can… I… help… you?"

A voice shouted out, "You bastard… you can't help me. You idiots are responsible for killing my wife and child. I went to buy a used car because I saw one of your stupid commercials. You're nothing but a bunch of liars. I'm going to rid the world of slime like you."

He came out of the shadows holding a six inch kitchen knife as he approached Kelby from the front.

Kelby reached for his gun in the back of his waistband but was unable to get it out before the man lunged at him. Kelby stumbled and went down and the man was standing over him.

"GO! GO! GO!" screamed Miller into the mic.

"Beg for your life, you worthless scum. I want to hear you beg before I kill you," said the man dressed in black.

Just as he lunged to stab Kelby, Miller screamed, "Halt, police!" When the suspect didn't stop, Miller shot him three times in the back. Roberts came in from the side door with SWAT coming in the through the service department. As the man fell, he dropped the knife. Miller kicked it away from the suspect and turned him over. He was dead.

Miller went over to Kelby who was still on the ground.

"Are you okay, partner?... Bill...?"

Bill Kelby lay unresponsive.

"MEDICS!" Miller shouted. His partner was in a state of shock. The ambulance pulled up, went over to Kelby, gave him oxygen, took off his jacket, took off his tie, removed his knife resistant vest, and opened his shirt. His blood pressure was dangerously high along with his pulse.

"Bill, it's Joe... you're okay. He's dead. The... guy... is... dead."

"I... I... couldn't get my gun out of my waistband. Jesus, he was standing right there... on top of me, ready to stab me."

"It's okay. Roberts and I were covering you."

"He's in shock. We need to take him to the hospital now for evaluation," said the paramedic.

Captain Reno showed up as they were putting Kelby on a gurney.

"I'd like to ride along," said Miller to Captain Reno.

"Go ahead," Reno replied.

"Squad 43 to Base."

"Base bye."

"We have a male approximately 30 years old, 6',
about 175 pounds, BP 180/110, pulse 120. He was
part of a stakeout where he was nearly killed by the
perpetrator. He appears to be in shock. We have
administered oxygen."

"ETA to the hospital?"

"Ten minutes.

"Give him 2 mg of Ativan and recheck vitals. His
blood pressure is too high. I don't want him to stroke
out," said the Emergency Room Doctor.

"Roger."

Kelby got the medication and it brought his BP
down to 140/80.

When Kelby got to the E.R., Miller told him what
happened.

"I think we just need to let him rest. He had a
great shock. The medication will cause him to relax.
He should be good to go in about four to six hours,"
said the E.R. doctor.

Miller went over to his partner, grabbed his arm
to give him a reassuring squeeze, and said, "You rest.
I'll see you soon."

With that, Miller left and went back to the
dealership to meet with Internal Affairs and do the
report. The coroner had just arrived and they were
loading the body in the wagon.

"What happened?" asked Reno.

"He had trouble getting his gun out of his
waistband. The guy was on him like stink on shit. He

was already sweating and upset that he was the bait... Damn, I should have been it given how he felt."

Captain Reno put his hand on Miller's shoulder and replied, "Nobody should have to be the bait... Come on, let's finish up what we need to do here and go see Bill."

———————————

Previously published by CaféLit

Murder at the Los Angeles Zoo

Miller walked in expecting to see Kelby, sitting at his desk but the chair was empty. Kelby usually got in before him and made the first pot of coffee of the day unless they were on a stakeout together. No Kelby, no coffee. Miller walked over and started the pot. He always had trouble opening the bag of grounds without using his Swiss Army knife while Kelby was an expert at it. He had been doing it since he was a kid; getting up, and making the brew for his folks before heading off on his paper route.

Something wasn't right. *Where's Bill?*

The water stopped flowing on the grounds and Miller poured himself a cup and went over to his desk. *Still no Bill.* Captain Reno was in his office but Miller didn't want to bother him, especially if Bill was running late due to traffic.

Miller received the coroner's report from the shooting at the Used Car Lot a few days before. It was time for him to finish his report. He had already been interviewed and cleared by Internal Affairs as it being a good shoot. "It was unfortunate Detective Joe Miller had to use deadly force against the suspect," the Internal Affairs report began, "but it couldn't be avoided. The suspect was shot three times in the back because he refused Detective Miller's verbal commands to halt as he attempted to stab Detective Miller's partner, Detective Bill Kelby.

One of the bullets entered the suspect's heart which killed him instantly. One bullet entered the spine and one bullet entered the liver."

Miller read and reread the report. He killed the suspect to save the life of his partner. It *was* a good shoot. It ended the only way it could have. The other alternative would have been to have had his partner stabbed to death. Miller sipped his coffee and thought pensively about the situation and what Dr. Delmonico said. *He was normal at one time and suffered a tremendous loss which pushed him over the edge…* The man needed help… not three bullets in the back but the situation that developed was beyond his control. He had to shoot to kill.

"Joe…"

Miller heard his name and looked up to see Captain Reno standing in front of him. He was so deep in thought he never heard him approach.

"Joe… I'd like you to step into my office."

"Bill isn't here yet," he said as he rose from his chair.

"I know. I gave him some time off. It looks as though you could use some too. I could give this new case to two other detectives and you could go home and get some rest."

"No, I'm fine," Miller responded.

"I suspect you're not but for now I have to believe you as I have a case for you and I'd like you to temporarily team-up with someone you've worked with in the past."

"Who might that be?" said Miller curiously.

Miller followed Captain Reno into his office and saw Marlene Jones sitting there in a tasteful blue suit, white blouse, and blue high heel shoes. It was a far cry from the hooker's outfit he saw her in the last time they met.

"Hello," she said waiting for a response.

"Hello. I thought you just worked Vice and Narcotics," Miller said.

"I do but I was asked to fill in here while Kelby was out," Jones replied.

"Captain, come on… what's going on with Bill?"

"He needed time off to get over the trauma of the last few days. His blood pressure is up and he is having trouble sleeping. During the time he's out, he has to have some sessions with Dr. Delmonico. Dr. D. will clear him with the Department to come back fit for duty. He needs to come to grips with what happened. Are you sure you don't need the same thing? The two of you went through a traumatic situation."

"Bill more than me… No, I'm good. So what's the case you want Officer Jones and me to work on together?" asked Miller.

"I need you to go to the Los Angeles Zoo, specifically go to Administration, and see the Director of Zoo Relations. There's been a murder at the white rhino enclosure," said Captain Reno.

"How did it happen?" asked Miller.

"It looks like the enclosure cleaner was stabbed to death by the rhino but there are some inconsistencies here," said Captain Reno.

"Such as?"

"The coroner on the scene reported the stabbing was a downward motion but a rhino would stab upwards," stated Captain Reno.

"Not to be a smart ass, but what if the assistant was down on all fours checking something out like its leg or underbelly of the animal or picking up droppings and it suddenly got angry and bolted," said Miller.

"Possible," said Captain Reno.

"May I interject?" inquired Jones.

"Yes of course," replied Reno.

"It is unlikely that the white rhino did this because even though rhinos as a species can be aggressive, the white rhino is calmer. I learned that on a zoo tour. They respond to threats by running away, not charging."

"So if it isn't the white rhino, who or what did it?" asked Miller.

"That's for you and Officer Jones to find out. Forensics has been out there digging around in the pen since this early morning when the body was found. The muddy footprints found near the body did not fit the enclosure cleaner and there were no footprints near the body," replied Captain Reno.

"You think the body was dumped there but was

killed somewhere else? Was anything stolen from the body, for example a ring, watch, or wallet?" asked Miller.

"Nothing was touched so robbery wasn't the motive," said Reno.

"Maybe the guy owed someone money... had some gambling debts maybe? Owed the mob perhaps?" asked Jones.

"No, he didn't gamble. We already checked into his vices and except for an occasional beer when the boys all met for drinks, he didn't smoke, drink, gamble, or run around with women or men," responded Reno.

"Ex-wife?" asked Miller.

"Nope."

"Sounds like a boring guy... so, why would someone off him?" said Jones.

"When I talked to his boss about his background outside work, he couldn't come up with a reason why someone would want him dead. He was a model employee who was about to be promoted."

"What about his co-workers?" asked Miller.

"That's what you're going there to find out because this doesn't make any sense." Reno shook his head. "You need to come up with a reason why a model employee with no vices was murdered today."

"You mentioned he was a model employee about to be promoted. I see one possibility. What about jealousy?" said Jones.

"That's for you to find out. Go to administration. Start there. And if it isn't a person you're after, then you have lots of four-legged suspects," stated Reno.

"Captain, do you have any idea how big the Los Angeles Zoo is and how many animals live there?"

"Excuse me, Joe, but it covers 133 acres, with more than 1,700 mammals, birds, amphibians, fish, and reptiles who live there," remarked Jones.

Both Miller and Captain Reno stared at her like she needed to give it a rest.

Miller continued, "Excluding the animals that couldn't have killed a human like birds, aquatics, most reptiles, and fish, you're talking about a lot of animals that *could* have plus their trainers, assistants, other enclosure cleaners, veterinarians, and vet techs and the entire administrative staff. You want Jones and me to go there and check out the *entire* zoo? All we know now was the white rhino more than likely didn't do it and it might have been a human being."

Captain Reno was about to say something when Miller interrupted.

"Plus, do you know how many people visit the zoo in a day? There are also the people who feed the animals too."

"All of that has been considered which is why the two of you need to get out there and survey the situation. Do what you do best and nose around," said Reno.

"Is the body still there or did the coroner take it away?" asked Miller.

"No, the coroner hasn't removed it, yet."

"Come on Jones… it's time for you to get your feet wet. Perhaps literally. Let's pick-up some protective shoes before we go."

Bill Kelby tossed and turned in bed back and forth, culminating with a blood curdling scream in his sleep. His wife, Joanna, reached over and shook him but he didn't respond. She had already gotten the kids up and off to school. The neighbor offered to drive them during this difficult time.

She sat on his side of his bed, grabbed him by the shoulders and yelled, "Bill, wake up. You're having a bad dream. You're home, in your own bed, and everything is okay."

Bill opened his eyes and sat up. He grabbed his wife and held her tight.

"It's okay. You're here… with me… at home," she said as she stroked his head.

"He was standing over me with a knife, ready to kill me," Bill said as he continued clutching his wife.

Miller and Jones took Miller's car. She didn't know if she should make small talk or not. Their last assignment they were thrown together, literally, with him posing as a John and her as a prostitute to catch a man who was killing prostitutes and emasculating

Johns. It was close but they got the guy and he was put away for a long time.

Miller didn't know what to say to her either. His partner had been traumatized badly. He hoped that Kelby could get over this but Miller was worried. They have been together five years, five long years… a lifetime in this business. They investigated murders, discovered who did them, and brought most of the perpetrators to justice, most… not all. Sometimes it was them or us. That's what the last case had been: life or death.

Kelby got up, showered, and left for therapy. It had been three days since… since the man nearly killed him at the Used Car Lot. Captain Reno told him to take some time off to get his head on straight. Time… time was his enemy not his friend. He kept seeing the perpetrator's face… the six inch knife… and hearing his partner calling his name.

"Bill, talk to me," said Dr. Delmonico. "I've known you and Joe a long time. The two of you have been through a lot together. He had your back and you've had his. I've helped both of you profile many suspects. I understand you've been through a trauma. It's the same type of trauma soldiers go through in battle. It's called Post Traumatic Stress Disorder. But Bill, I can't help you if you won't talk to me," said Dr. Delmonico.

"What do you want me to say?" he responded angrily.

"What do you feel now? What did you feel then?"

"Frightened. Damn it, I was scared shitless. I panicked when I couldn't get my gun out of my waistband and the killer was standing there, over me, with a six inch kitchen knife, ready to stab me, telling me I should beg for my life," replied Bill.

"Rationally you knew your partner, SWAT, and another detective were there. But you can't help how you feel staring into the face of a man who wanted you dead," said Dr. Delmonico.

"I've been in tight situations with Joe before but this time I felt utterly alone. Logically, I *knew* Joe was there but *I* was face to face with the killer of two innocent men. This guy had nothing to lose by killing me. He lost his family and he blamed others for his loss. I could have been number three. My wife would have been without a husband and my kids would have grown up without a father. All of that was going through my mind."

"Joe killed the suspect," said Dr. Delmonico.

"I heard Joe call to the suspect to drop the knife and when he didn't, Joe shot him three times. He fell to the right of me. Then Joe stood over me in the showroom calling my name. I couldn't even answer him. I was paralyzed with fear. Jesus, I had never been that scared before," replied Bill.

Dr. Delmonico paused and looked at Bill. He sat

back in his chair and asked, "So where do you want to go from here?"

"What do you mean, where do I want to go from here?" Bill retorted.

"*If* you go back to the Major Case Squad, you go back to the same type of cases that you and Joe have been investigating for years. Murders… mostly, but deranged, fucked-up people doing irrational things, nearly all of them murderers and them needing to be imprisoned for a very long time."

"*I know that*, but how do I get over this fear?"

"Maybe you don't. Maybe you have to learn to live with it and move on," stated Dr. Delmonico.

"That's your *answer*?" Bill turned and looked away.

"Did you expect me to do a dance that will free you of your fear? It doesn't work like that, Bill. Getting over trauma takes time. You have to look inside yourself and decide if you want to continue to be a detective with the Major Case Squad."

"Police work is all I know," replied Bill emphatically.

"There is always desk duty," stated Dr. Delmonico.

"I'd die if I were chained to a desk."

"Then by being in the field, you will run the risk of being in a situation like the one you were in, AND, this is the really important part, you have to be ready to go back and face whatever the situation is, because you are no good to anyone if you have it in your head that you or your partner may get shot. Then you will be lost, maybe forever. You can't second guess yourself. It has to come from the gut. It needs to be automatic. Los Angeles needs good detectives. Joe needs a partner he can rely on. But you have to be sure you can do the job. We can continue to meet whenever you need to but first you have to make the decision if you want to go back and be Joe's partner," replied Dr. Delmonico.

"There's no decision to be made. I was born to be a detective with the Los Angeles Police Department and to uphold the law. I must go to the range, practice handling my gun, and do whatever it takes to become the old Bill Kelby."

"Sounds like a great start. How about we meet the same time on Friday? You can update me on how you did at the range and how you're dealing with your feelings. Maybe you need to give Joe a call. I'm sure he's concerned."

"I will. Thanks Dr. Delmonico. I'll stop by the station and I'll see you here at 10 a.m. on Friday," said Kelby.

"Take some pictures over here," said Miller to the Crime Scene Investigator pointing to the area around the animal enclosure and where the body was found. "And I want a cast taken of these footprints and the animal prints."

"Animal prints?" asked the CSI technician.

"Yeah, because if the white rhino didn't do it,

then I need to figure out what animal did. Is it another four-legged animal that could have done it?"

Miller walked around the perimeter of the crime scene looking for clues while Jones followed him soaking up every little nuance of what he was doing. In the bushes, he saw something shiny and went over to it. It looked like a candy bar wrapper. Miller yelled to the CSI tech to take a picture of it and bag it. He gingerly walked around the area where the wrapper was. Another shoeprint was found. It appeared to be a man's shoe, size 12 or 13.

"Cast this, will you?" asked Miller. "When will you have the evidence processed?" he said to the technician.

"Come by the lab this afternoon and I will have something for you then."

"Thanks," replied Miller.

The body was about to be loaded into the coroner's van when Miller and Jones walked over. Miller asked for the sheet to be pulled back. There wasn't much left of this guy's midsection. Jones turned white but kept her composure. It was time for them to head to the Administration building. Miller had it in his head that the suspect was a tall man with large feet but that profile had been wrong before. It could be a shorter stockier man who just happened to have big feet. Unfortunately that could be the entire zoo staff for all he knew. It didn't mean he committed the crime, but he might have seen something because he was there. It could be he came to feed the rhino, saw the dead man, and ran off or it could have been the killer.

No promotions ever. All I have to look forward to is cleaning animal enclosures and look at what that bastard did. That idiot kissed ass and got a promotion. I'm as good as Johnny was with the animals if not better. I should have been promoted too. Well, I showed them. I'll show them all. Let them think the animals killed the enclosure cleaner. Johnny wasn't the only one who deserved to be promoted. I applied for multiple positions. I love hanging out with the animals but I'm tired of picking up poop. Twenty years of cleaning crap. Let the new kids do it and get their hands dirty for a while but they don't want to. They went to college. They got Vet Tech degrees. Well, they should start at the bottom and work their way up like I did. I'm tired of getting a raise, saying I did a good job, but no promotion. Maybe I should have killed the head of personnel, not an animal enclosure cleaner like myself. Well, it doesn't matter now. What matters is that I should get the open position. It's rightly mine. It's time to plan the next murder if I don't get it. I'll kill them all if I have to in order to get what's rightly mine....

"So?" asked Miller to the Zoo Administrator. "Had there been any death threats against the animal enclosure cleaner?"

"Johnny… nah… couldn't ask for a nicer guy. He was about to be promoted."

"Promoted? To what?" asked Jones.

"To Assistant Vet Technician. He had been around here forever and knew more about the animals than the Techs with degrees. Sometimes *they* would ask him what was wrong if an animal wasn't eating or pooping, and he knew. There wasn't anything the guy didn't know."

"How does a guy who was a well-loved person end up dead?" asked Miller.

"I said, Well-loved by the animals," replied the Administrator firmly.

"You mean the two-legged kind not so much?" asked Miller.

"Your words not mine."

"Come on… cut the crap. Was he or wasn't he liked by his co-workers?" replied Miller.

"No… he wasn't," stated the Administrator.

"Were there threats?" asked Jones.

"Not exactly."

"What the hell does that mean?" said Miller. "Stop beating around the bush!"

"Management loved him… coworkers not so much. The animals were really happy with him. He could make a sick animal eat and / or poop by coming over and giving medicine unlike some of the techs who go by the book and when an animal doesn't react, they don't know what to do."

"So Johnny got promoted to assistant technician

163

and you think another employee, maybe another enclosure cleaner, could have offed him because this person was jealous?" said Miller.

"Hard to say... he kissed a lot of butts to get the promotion. The zoo isn't too keen on promoting people without degrees just on experience alone, so the other enclosure cleaners were not happy to see him get promoted. All *they* had to look forward to were the yearly raise and increased benefits. For them they would always be picking up poop," replied the Administrator.

"There was no other job they could promote to?" asked Jones.

[4]"Since it's a city job, they would have to wait for an opening in another department and test for it like anyone else. The only thing that would go with the person was the seniority."

"It sounds like anyone that walked on two legs hated him," said Joe.

"That about summed it up," replied the Administrator.

"Envy... the oldest motive to kill," said Jones.

"Let's go back to the office and see what the CSI people have for us," said Miller.

---

[4] This is a true story: In Los Angeles, I knew a man in the 1990s that cleaned the elephant enclosures for years and wanted to do something else but he had to test to get out of his position. He wanted get into the Bureau of Sanitation and be a Street Sweeper. (I will refrain on making a personal comment here.)

It was quiet on the ride back. Jones wasn't sure what to say so she just blurted out, "You could talk to Dr. Delmonico about what he thinks of this person. Are you interested in consulting him?"

"Sounds like a great idea."

"Good afternoon, Joe. I recognize this lady with you but I can't remember her name."

"Good afternoon Dr. Delmonico. This is my partner, Marlene Jones. She's filling in for Bill until he gets back," said Miller.

"We did meet on another case. It had to do with a man killing prostitutes and emasculating Johns."

"Good memory, Doc," said Jones.

"Well what can I do for the both of you? I hope it is something less problematic."

"'Fraid not, Doc. So how common would it be for someone to get so angry that another person gets a promotion from being an animal enclosure cleaner to an assisatant vet tech position that he would kill the victim because of said promotion?" asked Miller.

"Enraged… the word is 'enraged'," emphasized Dr. Delmonico. "It can cause a normal person to lose perspective and do something he usually wouldn't do. I wonder who else he envied. I wouldn't want to be in their shoes right now. Are you sure there aren't any other motives? Maybe the guy was a gambler and was killed for owing the wrong people money. Or he used drugs and he owed these people money to continue his habit."

"We have already considered these possibilities and it definitely isn't anything like you suggested," said Miller.

"What kind of person was he? Nice, abrasive, wonderful, hateful?" asked Dr. Delmonico.

"The animals loved him. People, not so much," replied Jones.

"So he pissed people off. What, he had an attitude?... How much of an attitude can you have picking up animal poop?"

"The attitude could have been, ha ha, you dumb bastards. I'm being promoted. Nah, nah, no more scooping poop for me. All *you* guys are ever going to be are enclosure cleaners," said Miller.

"So, he was obnoxious. He bragged. I'm not a pooper scooper any more. You are. Ha, ha for you. So I assume this caused your person to snap. He couldn't deal with his job anymore and rather than leave and look elsewhere which is what a normal person would do, he took his rage out and killed the person he was in competition with. He now is thinking he can have this job or he'll have to kill again to secure his position in case anyone else would get it over him. You need to draw him out," stated Dr. Delmonico.

"Draw him out?" asked Jones.

"Yes, draw him out. Someone on the outside must be promoted to the position. This guy won't be able to handle the frustration and will be drawn out and try to kill again. I know someone who could be the pigeon but I have to see if he's willing to do it. I'll get back to you," replied Dr. Delmonico.

"Thanks for coming back today, Bill, to talk to me. How do you feel?" asked Dr. Delmonico.

"Pretty good. I went to the range, shot my gun, and practiced putting it in and retrieving it out of my waistband and holster."

"Good. Now I want to run something by you and before you tell me to go and stick it, I want to throw you back into action. You trust me, right?" asked Dr. Delmonico.

"Yeah, I guess," said Bill hesitantly.

"Miller and Jones are working on a case. They need someone no one has seen before to go in undercover to the Los Angeles Zoo and pose as a person who has come from another zoo to be promoted from an animal enclosure cleaner to assistant vet tech. They believe the killer will become enraged and will try to kill again because he wants this job. We need to test the theory."

"You want me to be the pigeon AGAIN," shouted Bill at the top of his voice.

"Basically… yes," replied Dr. Delmonico matter-of-factly.

"No offense, Doc., but I think *you're* nuts," Bill stood up and headed for the door.

"You want to be cured of your fear. Correct? I call this facing your fear or baptism by fire. It would be set-up like the Used Car Lot case. You would be assigned an animal enclosure to clean. The announcement will be made that you are getting the deceased person's job because of your stellar record at another zoo. The place will be swarming with SWAT plus Miller, Jones, Roberts, and other Major Case Squad detectives. Then it becomes a wait and see game," said Dr. Delmonico waiting for the no to come.

"I'm sorry Doc, but I can't do this," answered Bill.

You need to face your fears or maybe… just maybe you *want* to sit behind a desk for the rest of your career."

"You know that's not true."

"Then you need to do this," replied Dr. Delmonico.

"I… don't… know," stuttered Bill.

"If you don't do this, you will regret it for the rest of your life," said Dr. Delmonico sadly.

"Okay, let me talk with Joe, get the low down on the case, and go from there."

"I can't ask for anything more."

Kelby walked into the Major Case Squad room. Everyone came over and shook his hand. He was greeted warmly by all the guys, including Captain Reno, Miller, and Jones.

"I understand you need a pigeon again," said

Kelby. He looked at Miller and then looked at the floor. He shuffled his feet as he talked.

"Yeah, and I'm sorry. We need to flush the guy into the open. You know your cover?" asked Miller wishing it could be him and not his partner.

"Couldn't you have gotten me a position of authority? Do I have to clean animal enclosures?" said Kelby.

"Hopefully no but you have to make it look like you are," replied Miller.

"Look I'm not thrilled being at the zoo in the first place. The kids like it. I can't stand the smell." His eyes were already running at the thought of all the bad smells at the zoo.

"Don't take your allergy meds and hopefully you won't smell anything," said Miller trying not to smile.

"Funny... very funny. *I'm* not laughing."

Kelby wore a microphone taped to his chest just under his uniform. It was a hot spring day and he was sweating buckets from the heat and being so nervous. He had a water bottle with him and took a few gulps.

"Bill, testing one, two three," said Miller.

"I read you," replied Kelby.

"Roberts, you there?" asked Miller.

"10-4."

"Peters, are you around?"

"Yes."

"Captain Reno?"

"I'm here."

"SWAT Captain?" asked Miller.

"Yes, SWAT is in place. Five officers are all over that cage like stink on sh… well you know."

"You know, SWAT Captain, that was almost funny," said Kelby.

"Bill," said Joe, "we need you to walk around, hum, chew gum, look like you are picking up animal doo doo. I'll get the administrative guy to approach you to make the official announcement but the news already went around throughout the zoo. If our killer is going to try to knock you off, it'll be now."

Son of a bitch. They are promoting a person from another zoo. Well it's time he bites the big one too. And they assigned him Misty the elephant. Ha. I'll get her all riled up.

"It's my pleasure to announce our newest member of the staff. Mr. Bill Kelby. He will be promoted from animal enclosure cleaner to assistant vet technician. He will be taking Johnny's place. We are deeply saddened about what happened to Johnny. Of course our white rhino will have to be put down for being aggressive. Such a pity," said the Administrator.

"Thank you Administrator O'Hanion. I hope to make the zoo proud," replied Kelby.

Just then, Misty rose up on her two back legs screaming. She was being hit in the butt, and head with darts. The pain was too much. Misty started to stampede. Kelby pulled the Administrator out of the way, saw the perpetrator, and shouted, "Halt, Police."

Jensen screamed, "Screw you, screw all of you. That promotion was supposed to be mine." With that, he lunged at Kelby with a large knife similar to the one he faced at the Used Car Lot.

Kelby heard Miller scream, "Halt, Police."

Miller responded with, "Go, Go, Go," but this was Kelby's shoot. SWAT couldn't get a shot off. Miller ran to his partner with Jones and Roberts behind him.

Kelby aimed his gun and fired twice hitting the guy in the chest and abdomen killing him instantly.

Miller got to his partner out of breath just as Kelby lowered his gun. Miller said, "You okay partner?"

"Yeah, I'm better than okay… I'm back."

_____

Previously published by CaféLit

About the Author

Maxine lives in North Hollywood, California with her aquatic friends which include African dwarf frogs, tropical fish, and striped and tomato snails. She is disabled but she stays active by taking college classes at Los Angeles Pierce College mostly in English. Maxine has two A.A. degrees: one in Natural Science and one in Liberal Arts. Her goal is to pursue another A.A. in English but is waiting to see if she can get the classes she needs to do it.

She has self-published one book, entitled *Unglorious War, Revised Edition* and it is for sale on Amazon, B&N, Smashwords, Apple, and other platforms. Confessions Press in England published her second book on a limited run. The book is entitled *The Professionals 16, Meeting the Men of CI5*. The first limited two print runs sold out and they are considering doing a third run.

While she loves to write crime fiction and romance, Maxine has written futuristic, literary, dark and creepy, but not horror or gory stories, and a WWII historical story about a German doctor working on the side of the free French underground entitled, *Hiding Amongst the Gestapo* published by The Heartland Review Spring 2024 Edition.

Acknowledgements

Cover design by *Peter Shovlin* from an idea by *Maxine Flam*.

Some stories were proofread by *Gary K.* and *Dan N.*

And
   A shout-out to my computer technician, *Richard M.* who helped me at the last minute so I could finish this book on-time.

Like to Read More Work Like This?

Then sign up to our mailing list and download our free collection of short stories, *Magnetism*. Sign up now to receive this free e-book and also to find out about all of our new publications and offers.

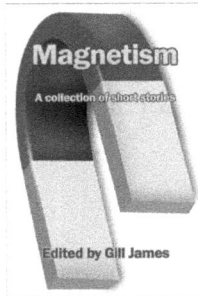

Sign up here:
http://eepurl.com/gbpdVz

Please Leave a Review

Reviews are so important to writers. Please take the time to review this book. A couple of lines is fine.

Reviews help the book to become more visible to buyers. Retailers will promote books with multiple reviews.

This in turn helps us to sell more books... And then we can afford to publish more books like this one.

Leaving a review is very easy.

Go to https://amzn.to/4ohvBfU, scroll down the left-hand side of the Amazon page and click on the "Write a customer review" button.

Other Writing by Maxine Flam

Unglorious War, Revised Edition

Major Thomas Harrison Smith is critically wounded while escaping
from a POW camp deep inside LAOS during the Vietnam War.
Stabilized by medical personnel, he is flown to Oahu, Hawaii for
surgery and rehabilitation. Emaciated, dehydrated, and half-dead from
torture and constant beatings, he meets Lt. Marla Bristol, a nurse-
therapist assigned to his case. During Major Smith's recovery, he and
Lt. Bristol fall in love and marry. The military wants Major Smith to do
another tour of duty. Major Smith agrees to return to Vietnam. Will he
see his beloved Marla again? Who is Lt. Anthony Lambello and what
part does he play in whether Major Smith returns from NAM?
Thomas and Marla are scared but each waits for the time they will be
reunited. Major Smith's faith is strong. Marla has doubts. Both look for
the day they will be permanently together again. God answers their
prayers, but is it the way that they hoped for?

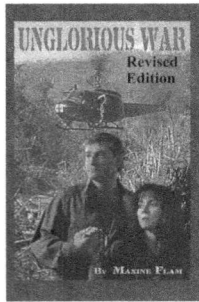

"I really enjoyed this book, and I recommend it highly to others
who enjoy good fiction, and especially to those who appreciate
historical fiction." *(Amazon)*

Order from Amazon:

Paperback: ASIN B0CSNCW3HV
eBook: ASIN B0CVH1KVYB

Other Publications by Bridge House

Feel-Good Stories
by Sarah Swatridge

A book to enhance your wellbeing and tug at your emotions.

An eclectic mix of heart-warming stories, full of memorable and quirky characters. Read about the heroic postie, the eccentric duke, a spoilt parrot, a true friend and a determined would-be husband. Perfect bite-sized reading with your favourite drink.

Enjoy Sarah Swatridge's uplifting *Feel-Good Stories*.

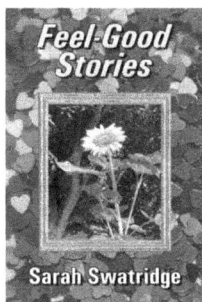

"A heart warming collection of short stories that do as the title suggests - make you feel good!" (*Amazon*)

Order from Amazon:

Paperback: ISBN 978-1-914199-62-2
Ebook: ISBN 978-1-914199-63-9

The Post Box Topper Chronicles
by *Dawn Knox*

A boring post box. Five knitters. Can one woman convert a post box into a work of artistic genius?

Vera Twinge is a natural leader. As chairperson of the newly-formed Creaping Bottom Post Box Topper Society, she's determined to make a splash in the village's High Road with a stunning new post box topper for each month. But she's constantly obstructed by an unscrupulous journalist, an insulted hairdresser and a possible mass murderer. Urging her society members on to create more ingenious toppers, Vera refuses to be defeated. But with negative reports in the local newspaper, a revenge haircut and the threat of alien invasion, Vera wonders if she is up to the task.

Will Vera and her post box topper society expose the strange happenings in Creaping Bottom and keep their beloved post box an object of beauty?

"The Post Box Topper Chronicles by Dawn Knox was a truly delightful read." (*Amazon*)

Order from Amazon:

Paperback: ISBN 978-1-915762-12-2
Ebook: ISBN 978-1-915762-13-9

Chapeltown Books

And I Said...
by Linda Morse

And what she said is paramount. These accounts from one person's point of view each contain at least as much story as a long novel or a feature film.

The monologues, and one experimental play, have already been performed. Here is your opportunity to revisit them if you have seen them and/or have had a go at preforming them yourself. Which will you choose? The story of the young woman who struggles with juggling home schooling and remote working during Lockdown? Or the one about the bride who never does manage to own her wedding dress? Perhaps the strange conversation that happened on a train that was held up? There are so many intriguing pieces to consider.

And I Said… is a thought-provoking collection by gifted playwright Linda Morse.

"a delightful collection of random monologues." (*Amazon*)

Order from Amazon:
Paperback: ISBN 978-1-914199-62-2
eBook: ISBN 978-1-914199-63-9

www.ingramcontent.com/pod-product-compliance
Ingram Content Group UK Ltd.
Pitfield, Milton Keynes, MK11 3LW, UK
UKHW040744240825
462207UK00005B/32